THE SILENT SUMMER

CAITLIN GOERLICH

Visit my website at www.caitlingoerlich.com
Cover Designer: Jaycee DeLorenzo, Sweet 'N Spicy Designs, https://www.
sweetnspicydesigns.com/
Editor: Jovana Shirley, Unforeseen Editing, www.unforeseenediting.com

ISBN-13: 978-1-7369104-0-5

To Mom
Thank you for being my Mama-Coach.
I love you ❤

GRANDMA'S SUMMER HOUSE

"*I* love you," *says the seventeen-year-old girl sitting down near the bed while wearing her brown hair up in a messy bun, tears streaming down her cheeks.*

The frail woman, who lies on the hospital bed with tubes coming out of her nose, slowly moves her right hand up to rest it on her daughter's face and whispers, "I love you too, Ellie-Bear. Watch out for your dad and brother for me?"

Danielle nods her head as tears continue to fall, and she moves closer to the bed, so she can rest her head down on her mom's arm. She sobs when she hears one machine let out a long, high-pitched sound. Then, she turns her head to notice her mom's eyes are closed.

She's gone.

Her blue eyes shoot open, and her chest moves up and down. She looks around the room and sighs, knowing she had the dream again. The same dream she's had every night for the past two weeks since her mom passed away in front of her. *It's never going to go away.*

"Dani?" she hears a low voice say.

She looks over to see her seven-year-old little brother standing at her door, holding his teddy bear close to his chest.

"Can I sleep with you?"

She smiles, moves over to make room on her bed, and opens her arms. He runs over, places his body in her arms, lying down, and rests his head on her shoulder while tightly holding on to his bear.

He stares up at her and asks the same question he asks every night, "Dani … why don't you talk anymore?"

Danielle looks down at him and shrugs her shoulders. She hasn't said a word in the last couple weeks. And she doesn't plan on talking anytime soon. They get comfortable and both close their eyes, knowing they have a long day ahead of them.

DANIELLE WATCHES the trees pass by as she leans her head against the window of the passenger door of her dad's car. She bites her lower lip and sighs.

"Sweetie?"

She turns to stare blankly at her dad.

"Are you sure you're okay with staying with Grandma this summer?"

She nods her head. *Anything to get away from this place.*

Her dad sighs as he continues driving down the highway toward his mom's house in Calm Beach, New Jersey, where Danielle and Jacob will spend their summer. It's the only thing he could think of. He knows it will be hard on them for a while, especially for Danielle.

DANIELLE NOTICES her dad making a right turn, and she watches the nice-sized beach houses pass by until they stop in front of the two-floor blue colonial beach house she knows so well. One -by - one, they step out of the car and look up at the front porch to see the gray-haired woman standing up from the chair, waiting for them with a smile.

"Hi, kids," she says as she walks down the porch steps to meet them.

"Grandma!" Jacob yells as he wraps his arms around her waist.

"Hi, Jacob!" She smiles as she returns the hug before looking at her son.

He walks over and gives her a kiss on her cheek. "Hey, Mom."

"Hi, John." She smiles as Jacob pulls away from her, and she glances over at Danielle. "How's she doing?"

"The same," he says with sadness in his voice.

Grandma places her hand on John's shoulder, giving it a slight squeeze, and then looks back at Danielle. "Hi, sweetie."

She smiles softly as she walks over to her and wraps her arms around her grandma's waist. Grandma returns the hug and gives her a soft kiss on her temple. Danielle pulls away, staring behind her at the house before walking up the porch steps and disappearing behind the front door.

"Thanks for doing this, Mom."

"I'd do anything for my grandchildren, John." She turns to him. "You might want to go. Don't want you to get stuck in traffic."

John nods in agreement and turns, bending down to give Jacob a hug. "You take care of your sister and Grandma, okay?"

"I will, Dad."

John lets him go and turns to give his mom a hug, "Tell Danielle that I love her and I'll call or text her when I get home."

"I will." She gives him one more squeeze before pulling away. "Have a safe drive home."

John nods and turns around, walking toward his car. He opens the driver's side, and as he's about to step into it, he hears quick footsteps. Turning around, he sees Danielle running over to him. He opens his arms, and she wraps her arms around him. He returns the hug and strokes her hair with his left hand.

"I love you, baby girl," he whispers in her ear. "Everything's going to be okay."

Danielle nods against his shoulder before she pulls away.

"I'll call or text you later." He kisses her forehead.

She steps back. He gives her one more smile before stepping into his car, and closes the door behind him. He puts his seat belt on and turns the key to start the engine. He looks out the window and raises his hand to wave before pulling away from the curb.

I love you, Daddy.

Jacob walks up to stand next to her and takes her hand. Danielle looks down, giving him a slight smile. No matter how bad things get, Jacob always seems to be able to keep a smile on her face, and she loves him even more for that reason.

"Come on, kids," they hear their grandma say after a few moments of silence. "We need to get you two settled in."

Danielle and Jacob both turn around. Jacob lets Danielle's hand go as they follow their grandma into the house, where they will live for the next couple months. Danielle was kind of excited to get away for a while, as she didn't want to hang around her hometown with people who constantly asked her if she was okay.

Their family lives in a small town called Skystead in north New Jersey, where everyone knows everyone. She was born and raised in the town and became the girl everyone loved and watched out for. Danielle always compared herself to Rory from her favorite show, *Gilmore Girls,* who was always watched and cared for in Stars Hollow.

Danielle recently graduated high school with straight A's. She and her mom were very close, as the entire family is. Everyone in Skystead remembers just how much, so they would check up on her all the time after her mom died. But since then, she never lets anyone in or talks to anyone by voice and was getting tired of the attention and pitying looks she received.

So, with them staying at their grandma's house, she hopes it will help her. Help her have a fresh start here where she can finally find some peace.

2
THE BEACH

*D*anielle is sleeping on her side with the sheet over her and her head on the pillow, but there's movement on her bed. She flutters her eyes open and moves her eyes over to see Jacob jumping up and down, looking at her.

"Wake up!" Jacob shakes her, but he sees her eyes are open, so he stops. "Good. You're awake. Grandma said that you can take me to the beach."

Oh, great ... I can't say no to him. Well, I guess we're going to the beach.

She smiles and nods her head in agreement as she looks at him. Jacob claps his hands excitedly, and he jumps off the bed. He runs out of Danielle's room. She shakes her head and stares up at the ceiling, giggling before getting up so she can get ready.

DANIELLE STANDS with her arms crossed as she watches Jacob playing in the sand. She smiles as he packs some sand together while building a sand castle. But the next thing she knows, she's being bumped into by a hard body, and she falls to the ground. She groans, holding her arms out to break her fall.

"Oh man … I'm sorry," she hears a guy's voice say as he reaches his hand out toward her. "I should've been watching where I was going."

She stares at the hand before grabbing it, and the person helps her stand up. Once she's standing, she lets go of the hand and looks down at her pants, brushing the sand off them. She looks back up to notice the guy is around her age and is an inch taller than her with shaggy, spiky brown hair and dark brown eyes, which are staring back at her.

"I'm Trevor," he says, holding his hand out. "What's your name?"

Danielle takes his hand and shakes it. She opens her mouth to say something but closes it, remembering she doesn't talk anymore. Then, arms are wrapped around her waist, and she lowers her eyes down to find Jacob staring up at her.

"Are you okay, Dani?"

She nods.

"Good," says Jacob before removing his arms. He looks up at Trevor. "Who are you?"

"Trevor," he answers with a smile and looks back at Danielle. "So … what's your name?"

Danielle looks down.

Jacob knows she won't say anything, so he looks at Trevor and speaks for her, "Her name's Danielle. She doesn't talk."

"Oh … I get it. I was shy, too, my first time coming here."

"She's not shy," Jacob says when he sees a tear fall down Danielle's cheek. "She hasn't talked since our mommy died a few weeks ago."

"Oh, I didn't mean to …" Trevor says but doesn't have time to finish as Danielle shakes her head before running away from them. "Wait."

He tries to stop her, but it is too late. She is already gone from their eyes. He looks down and sees Jacob still standing there, looking lost as he stares toward the direction his sister ran off without him.

Good job, Trevor.

"So, uh … ya want me to take you home?" asks Trevor, holding his hand out for Jacob.

"Okay," says Jacob as he takes his hand. "And my name is Jacob!"

TREVOR USES his pointer finger to press the doorbell. He glances down to Jacob, who stares up at him with a smile. They hear the door opening. Trevor looks at it and notices a familiar older woman, who he has seen around town, looking at the two of them in surprise.

"Um, hi," he nervously says. "I'm Trevor. I, uh … was at the beach and ran into Danielle and Jacob. I thought I would bring Jacob back since Danielle ran off."

"Ah, so you're the one," Grandma Marie sighs and shakes her head and then looks at Jacob. "Sweetie, can you go inside, please?"

Jacob nods his head and lets go of Trevor's hand. "See you around."

"Yeah … sure, buddy," Trevor says as Jacob walks into the house and then looks back at the grandmother. "Um, … I guess I should go."

He starts to turn around but hears the gray-haired woman talk, "Listen, my granddaughter and grandson have been through a lot these past few weeks. I've seen you around town, and I know you're a good kid, so if you want, you can go up and talk to her."

"I don't think …" he says.

But the woman, who he now remembers is known as Grandma Marie around town, interrupts, "She's been crying since she ran back here. Because she misses her mom and is afraid to let anyone in. But also, I think she believes she made herself look like a fool to you." She shrugs her shoulders. "Call it a grandma's intuition."

Trevor raises his right eyebrow. "But she didn't."

"Then, go tell her that, or she'll lock herself in that room for the entire summer. And that isn't the point of them staying here."

"But we just met. I wouldn't know what to say to her."

"All I ask is …" Grandma Marie starts to say but pauses before continuing, "For you to talk to her. I don't care what about. I need her to not hide away all summer."

"Yes, ma'am," he agrees after seeing the concern she has for her granddaughter.

TREVOR STANDS in front of a light-gray door.

He shakes his head. *What am I supposed to say? I met this girl for, like, a second.*

He sighs, knowing he has no choice. *Here goes nothing.*

Trevor raises his hand and knocks on the door. No answer. He leans forward, pressing his ear up against the door and can hear crying on the other side. He moves his hand down to the door-knob, turning it to find it unlocked so he slowly pushes the door open. He walks in and quietly closes the door. He turns to see a queen-sized bed with Danielle crying on it.

As he saunters over to the bed, he whispers, "Hey … you okay?"

Danielle freezes when she hears the voice. She looks up from her pillow, and her eyes widen when she sees it's the guy from the beach. *What is he doing here?* She puts her head back down and turns it the other way.

"Hey," says Trevor as he sits on the edge of the bed. "You don't have to be afraid of me."

She turns her head and stares at him. He smiles. He doesn't understand what comes over him, but he moves his hand up and rests it against her cheek. With the pad of his thumb, he wipes away the tears that have fallen down her cheek. Danielle widens her eyes and bites her lower lip as she enjoys the touching moment.

"Now, do you think we can start over?"

Trevor pulls his hand away. Danielle thinks about it and nods with a smile.

"I'm Trevor." He puts his hand out toward her.

She rolls halfway over, so she's now lying on her side, and she reaches her hand out to shake his. She then leans over to grab her smartphone. Opening up the Notes app, she types.

I'm Danielle.

He reads it and looks at her. "It's nice to meet you, Danielle."

He seems nice. Cute too. Maybe I'll enjoy this summer more than I thought.

3

THE BAD BOYS OF CALM BEACH

"*D*o you like Trevor, Dani?"

Danielle looks over at Jacob, surprised, and shrugs her shoulders.

"He seems cool," he says. "He said he would hang out with me anytime I wanted to."

She smiles and reaches for her phone, typing.

Do you want to go to the beach to see if he's there?

Jacob stands up from the couch, nodding his head excitedly. Danielle laughs as she stands up and grabs his hand before they walk out of the house.

DANIELLE AND JACOB WALK HAND in hand along the beach, looking for Trevor. But suddenly, two muscular guys, wearing backward baseball caps, jump in front of them. They step back and see the guys smirking at them.

"Well, well, well, who is this hottie?" One of them licks his lips as he runs his eyes up and down Danielle. "I'm Mark, and this here is my friend Ray."

Ray reaches forward to take her hand. "Hey, baby, you want to come home with me?"

Danielle yanks her hand away. She grabs Jacob's hand and starts walking backward, away from them as her eyes widen and arms start to shake.

"Aw, don't be afraid." Mark walks closer to her. "We're not going to hurt you."

"Leave my sister alone!" Jacob exclaims.

Ray laughs. "Aw, is this your little protector?"

Mark pushes Jacob to the ground, which causes Jacob and Danielle to separate their hands. Mark walks closer to Danielle, reaching his hand behind her to touch her butt. Ray moves closer, taking her hand, pulling her close to him. She tries pushing them away, but they are too strong. She closes her eyes, waiting for whatever will happen next.

But then she doesn't feel anyone on her. She opens her eyes and sees both Ray and Mark on the sand, groaning. She raises her eyes to see Trevor standing over them.

"Never—and I mean, never—touch her or anyone like that again!" He shakes his head as he glares at the two of them with anger. "And you never push a kid who's younger than you down again. You two are worthless pieces of shit. Get lost."

They stand up quickly and walk off, muttering to each other. Trevor can hear every word they say, and it takes a lot for him not to run after them, but he shakes his head. He turns around to see Danielle staring at him, and he walks to her.

"Hey ... are you okay?"

She stares at him, not knowing the answer to his question. It was one of the scariest moments that's ever happened to her. She bites her lower lip.

"Danielle?" He tries to look in her eyes but she keeps staring right ahead at him, so he asks, "Do you need a hug?"

Trevor's not sure what to do, so he asked the one question that he hoped would have her open up to him. She stops staring straight ahead and nods her head as tears form in her eyes. He smiles softly and opens his arms. Danielle walks close to him and rests her head against his chest as he wraps his arms around her waist. He rubs her back.

"Everything's going to be okay," he whispers in her ear and she nods against his chest.

Jacob stands up from the sand, wiping his clothes off, and looks over to notice Trevor and Danielle hugging. He smiles, knowing there's a chance she might open up to Trevor but it might take a while. He's hoping to get his sister back, the one before their mom died.

"Is everything okay?" he speaks up, which causes them to separate.

Danielle nods as she wipes her tears away and gives Jacob a reassuring smile.

"You okay, buddy?" Trevor looks at Jacob with concern. "They pushed you pretty hard."

"I'm fine. As long as she's okay."

She gives him a thumbs-up. Jacob knows she's trying to be strong for him. He's smart for his age, and he's always looking out for Danielle.

Trevor can tell she doesn't want to talk about what happened, so he changes the subject, "So ... what are you guys doing back at the beach today?"

"Oh, we came looking for you," Jacob answers. "I wanted to

hang out with you. The house is so boring! So, I asked Danielle, and she suggested we come search for you on the beach, so here we are."

"Oh, really?" He grins and winks at Danielle. "You got a thing for me already, huh?"

Danielle's mouth hangs open. Trevor starts laughing, shaking his head.

"I was kidding." He laughs again. "But sure, I'd love to hang out with you guys."

"Yay!" Jacob claps excitedly but stops when he raises his eyebrow. "Who were those guys who were bothering us?"

Danielle looks at Trevor with interest. Trevor shrugs his shoulders, thinking of a way to explain Mark and Ray to them.

He sighs before speaking,

"Let's just say, they are known as the bad boys of Calm Beach." He shrugs his shoulders. "They like to play girls, trash places, and pick on those who are younger than them. I hate those guys, as most of the town does, but they also hate me. In the end, I'm always the one who puts them down. So, if they ever bother you again, come find me, and I'll handle it."

He gives Danielle a reassuring smile. She bites her lower lip, worried about seeing them again or having them find out she's in a vulnerable state and using that against her. But as she looks at Trevor, she can see that he's serious about if they ever do anything to her or Jacob, he'll take care of it. He's already their protector and even though she doesn't want to admit it, she has a crush on him even with them only meeting yesterday. And that scares her.

"So, what do you want to do?" Trevor looks at Jacob.

"I want to go to the aquarium down the street. We haven't been there since last year when we went with Mommy."

Danielle looks down and remembers that day. It was one of the best days they had as a family. It was summer, and they came down to visit their grandma. For a family day, they decided to spend the entire day at the aquarium. Worry-free.

"That was a fun day," Jacob whispers, teary-eyed. "I miss Mommy."

She walks over to Jacob, and he wraps his arms around her waist. Danielle strokes the back of his head, showing him she misses her too. Trevor stands to the side, watching them have their sister-brother moment. He can't imagine what it's like for them since he hasn't lost a loved one, but he can understand how hard it must have been for them to lose their mom.

4

THE AQUARIUM

*J*acob stares at the tank with amusement, as he's done since the moment they entered the aquarium. Trevor and Danielle watch while they walk side by side together, following Jacob as he moves on to another tank. Trevor doesn't quite understand how to talk to Danielle since she won't physically reply to him, but they're in a comfortable silence. She can tell he won't try to push her to talk, like her friends did back home. And even though they haven't known each other long, he's different from any of the other guys she's met.

"So … have any friends back home?" Trevor throws his head back in embarrassment at the question he asked and then looks at her. "I mean …"

Danielle puts her hand up to stop him as she giggles. Then, she reaches her right hand in her purse to take out her phone.

Yes. I have friends. They're cool and all, but can be overprotective, especially since my mom's passing. We live in a small town, and when I was born, I was the town's, I guess, golden girl, so they all looked out for me and knew how important my mom was to me. They ALL kept

asking me if I was OK for the past couple weeks, and that's why I
agreed to come here.
To get away from all that.

She stops typing and holds it out for Trevor to read it.

Then, he turns to her with a surprised expression. "Wow. I guess you're like Rory from that show *Gilmore Girls,* only her mom didn't pass away. And yes, before you ask, I know what *Gilmore Girls* is."

Danielle laughs as she puts her phone back into her purse. She raises her eyes to find Trevor still looking at her. He smiles before moving his eyes away, and they continue walking.

"Dani! Dani! Dani!" Jacob comes running toward them with excitement.

She turns to him, raising her right eyebrow, waiting for him to explain his excitement.

"Bobcat is still here!"

Danielle shakes her head and giggles. Jacob grabs her hand and drags her away over to a large tank. Trevor watches them at first, amused and confused, following them over to see them staring intently in a tank.

Jacob points at the tank. "See? He's still here."

Danielle smiles as she sees a large turtle sitting on a log, surrounded by pebbles, plants, and water, where there are some fish swimming around. Jacob taps on the glass. Bobcat slowly moves off the log, goes into the water, and swims over to the glass.

"Hey, Bobcat," he says.

With amazement, Trevor watches the interaction between the turtle and Jacob, leading him to ask, "Who is this big guy?"

Jacob looks at Trevor. "Last year, we found him up on the beach and called the Humane Society. They took care of him and then put him in the aquarium. His tank is connected to an outdoor area, so he can go out whenever he wants to! And since we found him, we could name him, so we named him Bobcat."

"That's awesome," Trevor says and looks at Danielle. "You were here last year?"

She moves her head up and down.

"Too bad we didn't run into each other."

Yeah. Too bad. I'm starting to really like him. He seems sweet. He's definitely cute, kind of funny, and comfortable to be around.

"Well, if it isn't the Washingtons." They hear a man's voice behind them, so they turn around to see the six-foot man with a buzz cut, wearing an aquarium staff shirt.

"Keegan!" Jacob runs over to him, wrapping his arms around him.

"Hey, little man," he says as he pulls away from the hug. "Hey, Dani."

Danielle smiles and nods her head once to him.

"She doesn't talk anymore"—Jacob looks up at Keegan—"ever since Mommy died."

"Oh, right. My mom told me about that." He moves his eyes from Jacob to Danielle. "And I'm sorry for your loss. Your mom was awesome, and I know how close you all were. I'm also sorry I couldn't make it to the funeral. There was a lot going on here. I couldn't get away."

He walks over to Danielle, holding his arms out. She walks into them and rests her head against his chest, wrapping her arms around his waist. Closing her eyes, she takes a breath. Trevor watches and can't help but feel a pang of jealousy, but he's not going to admit it.

Danielle pulls away, giving Keegan a smile, and he returns the smile before noticing Trevor standing there.

He puts his hand out. "Hey. I'm Keegan. Their cousin on their dad's side of the family."

Trevor sighs in relief as he shakes Keegan's hand. "Trevor. Their new friend."

Keegan nods and takes his hand back. "So, came to visit Grandma for the summer?"

"And Bobcat!" exclaims Jacob.

"Well, Bobcat missed you. Want to see him?"

"Yes!"

"All right." Keegan chuckles. "Dani, want to go?"

She motions her hand for them to go ahead without her. Keegan puts his hand on Jacob's shoulder and pushes him toward a door, and then they disappear behind it. Trevor and Danielle turn to stare at the tank, watching Jacob walk into it with Keegan closely behind him.

"Keegan seems cool."

Danielle nods in agreement. She looks around for a place to sit. She sees a bench and motions her head at it. Trevor agrees. They walk over and sit down. Once she sits down, she looks around, and goose bumps form on her arms.

Is this the bench?

She looks at the center of the bench and notices the four initials that are carved there—JW, DW, JAW, and finally SW, which stands for Sandy Washington, their mom. Danielle traces her finger over the carvings. She closes her eyes as she tries to hold in the tears, but it's not working, as one tear falls down.

Trevor looks at her, concerned. "Are you okay? What's wrong?"

She points to the initials and a little message that her mom wrote after signing it.

Trevor shifts his body as he gets a better view and reads it out loud, "*No matter what happens, I'll always be watching over you.*"

And the dam breaks. Tears fall down Danielle's cheeks. This is when Trevor realizes they were expecting her to die but didn't know when. Sandy Washington was sick and dying when they were here for their last summer together.

"She was sick, wasn't she?"

Danielle nods her head and opens her eyes. She stares up at the ceiling. Trevor slides over, so there's no space between them, and he puts his arm around her. She turns to rest her head against his chest, and he places his chin on top of it when she wraps her arms around him. And she cries. He wraps his other arm around her as he tries to comfort her the best he can.

"It's going to be okay," he whispers and kisses the top of her head. "Want to go home?"

She nods against him. Trevor carefully stands up with her and walks over to the tank. He taps on the glass, and Keegan and Jacob turn around to see Danielle in Trevor's arms. They sigh, knowing what probably happened and understand, so they come out from the tank.

"She found the bench, didn't she?" asks Jacob, looking down.

"Yes," Trevor answers. "She wants to go home."

"Okay," says Jacob and looks over at Keegan. "Bye, Keegan."

"Bye, little man." Keegan looks at Danielle. "I'll come over when I get some time off."

Danielle nods but doesn't let go of Trevor. She feels safe in his arms, and she never wants to let go of him. Trevor can tell how upset she is. Even though they just met, he knows he has to be there for her, and he plans to be.

5

THE FIRST DATE

Since the day at the aquarium a few days ago, Danielle hasn't wanted to leave the house. And no one has pushed her, not even Trevor. He comes over to the house giving, Danielle some company whenever Grandma Marie takes Jacob out.

The death of their mom doesn't seem as hard for Jacob as it is for Danielle, but he's still hurting. But his mom wouldn't want him to be; she'd want him to have fun, like kids are supposed to. Those were the last words his mom ever told him.

"I don't want you crying over me, Jacob," his sick mom said, looking at him. "I know Dani will do enough crying for the both of you. I want you to have fun because you're young. You'll always have time to cry." She reached out for his small hand. "But do me a favor? Watch out for your sister for me. She will need you even though you're only seven."

"I will, Mommy." He rubbed his watery eyes. "I love you. I won't forget you."

He always thinks back to that moment when he feels like he's going to crack, but he promised his mom that he'd always act like a kid and to have fun. So, that's what he will do.

DANIELLE AND TREVOR sit together on the couch, staring at the TV screen, which is playing a movie, but neither one of them knows what's going on. He doesn't mind hanging around, as he doesn't have anything else to do. He enjoys spending time with her. And if he wasn't with her, she would be on his mind.

He glances over at her.

She can sense him, but she doesn't look. A part of her doesn't want him to waste his summer around her. But he told her he didn't mind, so she left it at that. And another part of her is happy to have someone like him around. He doesn't push her into doing anything, and it makes her happy. She hasn't felt this kind of happiness since her mom was around. She can feel herself slowly coming back. Plus, he's not too bad to look at.

"So ... you want to do something after the movie?"

Danielle turns to Trevor and smiles. Maybe it is time for her to get out of the house, and going out with Trevor seems like a good idea, especially if it's just the two of them. She nods.

Trevor grins as he moves his hand over to hers, lacing them together before turning back to watch the movie. Danielle looks down to their hands and then back up to him. Every time he touches her or even looks at her, a bunch of butterflies flutter around in her stomach.

He makes me feel special. But ... I don't know if he feels the same. He's probably only being nice to me because he feels sorry for me.

Little does she know, Trevor does feel the same. He's had a couple of girlfriends before, but none of them gave him the feelings she gives him. They only wanted to go out with him for status, as his family has money and he's one of the most popular guys in town. He hasn't told Danielle about any of that. He wants to make sure if anything were to happen between them, it'd be because she likes him for him and not for money or popularity.

THE TV SCREEN IS BLACK, but neither moves from the couch. They are both in deep thought about each other and still aren't sure what they are feeling, so they stay silent. Neither realizes they're still holding hands and Trevor starts stroking the back of hers with his thumb.

He looks at her and breaks the silence. "Would you like to go to dinner with me tonight?"

Danielle looks at him, confused. Taking her hand from his, she reaches for her phone.

I thought we were going to hang out after the movie?

"We are," he says, "but it'll be near dinner-time, and I would like to take you out. And not just to the beach. I think you need to see more than just the beach. What do you say?"

She bites her lower lip, and then the corners of her lips go up while she nods in agreement.

"All right. You go change into something nice. I'll go run home and be back in an hour."

She nods. They both stand up from the couch. Danielle walks Trevor over to the door. He leans in to press his lips to her cheek before he opens the door and walks out. She reaches her hand up to her cheek, resting it there as she watches him walk away until she can't see him anymore. Danielle closes the door and turns around, running up to her room to search for what to wear. It's her first date ever, and she wants to wear something perfect.

DANIELLE SITS DOWN on the couch as she waits for Trevor to come back. She looks down at her outfit, questioning if it is too much or not enough. She's wearing a short-sleeved, flowy white dress that rests right above her knees with one-inch black heels, and she has a matching white clutch. She decided to let her long, wavy brown hair naturally curl itself. Before she can make any changes, she hears the front door open, and in walk Jacob and Grandma Marie.

"Hey, sweetie." Grandma Marie smiles at her. "Where's Trevor?"

"Did he leave?" Jacob looks at her with a worried expression. "Why did he leave? I wanted to see him! Is he coming back?"

She holds her hand up as she giggles and grabs her phone.

Trevor went home to change. He's taking me out to dinner tonight.

Grandma Marie grins. "Aw … is this your first date?"

Danielle nods, biting her lower lip.

"Trevor's a nice boy. I'm glad that you'll have your first date with him. And you look beautiful, sweetie."

Thanks, Grandma.

"Date?" Jacob moves his eyes from Grandma Marie to Danielle. "What's a date?"

"It's when two people go out by themselves," Grandma Marie tries to explain, "either to dinner, movies, or whatever seems like fun for them, and they get to know each other."

Jacob grows more curious. "Did Mommy and Daddy have dates?"

Danielle nods.

"Does that mean you'll marry Trevor?" he asks. Then, he exclaims, "When?"

Danielle coughs, and her eyes widen. She is too young to be thinking about marriage; plus, she just met Trevor. But she understands Jacob is only seven and doesn't get what's going on. She looks at her grandma, and before she can explain more to Jacob, the doorbell rings.

Danielle stands up from the couch and walks over to the door, opening it to see Trevor wearing a nice short-sleeved white shirt with a black jacket—buttons open—and black regular-fit jeans. He's holding a bouquet of colorful flowers.

"These are for you. I had some time to pick them up before I came back." He holds them out toward her and then runs his eyes up and down. "You look beautiful."

Her cheeks turn rosy and she accepts the flowers before moving to the side, letting Trevor walk in. She closes the door and holds her pointer finger up. She brings the flowers to the kitchen, putting them in a vase with water as Trevor steps into the living room.

"Oh, hi!" he says as he notices Grandma Marie and Jacob. "Have fun at the zoo?"

"Yeah! It was so much fun!" Jacob exclaims. "So, are you going to marry my sister?!"

"Wait … what?" Trevor turns to him with his mouth agape. "Where did that come from?"

"Well, you're taking my sister out on a date, and my parents went on dates," says Jacob as he moves his head to the side. "So, you're marrying my sister."

Grandma Marie looks at Trevor. "He doesn't really understand what a date is."

"Ohh." Trevor looks at Jacob. "Your sister and I are not getting married. It's too early to talk about that. We're going on our first date, where two people go out and get to know each other. Have some fun. Sometimes, it can be months or even years of dates before people decide to get married or not."

Danielle walks into the room with the vase and places it on the coffee table. She sees Jacob moving his head up and down. She overheard Trevor's explanation and hopes Jacob understands what a date is. She doesn't want him to expect Trevor to be around forever. It's only their first date. Who knows how it will go?

"You ready to go?" Trevor asks, and she nods her head "Great. We should go then. I'll bring her home around ten thirty. Is that okay?"

"No. You can stay out as long as you want." Grandma Marie smiles. "I trust that you will take good care of her. So, come back whenever. Not too late though."

Danielle stares at her grandma in shock. They always had to be back at a certain time. Even when they were with their parents. She'd always get worried if the family stayed out too late. This is new for her.

"Okay," says Trevor before taking Danielle's hand. "Let's go. Bye, Marie. Bye, Jacob."

Jacob waves. "Bye."

"Have fun, kids."

Danielle smiles at them before walking to the front door with Trevor. He opens the door, and they walk out. Danielle's eyes widen as she notices a black Mercedes sitting in front of her house. She looks back at Trevor, and he shrugs his shoulders. They walk down the porch stairs. She stares at the car as they reach it.

He can afford this?

Trevor reaches forward to open the passenger door. She smiles before getting in. She gazes around the inside. Danielle can't believe she's sitting in a Mercedes. She grabs the seat belt and pulls it around her, clicking it in as she continues to look around.

Trevor gets into the driver's seat and clicks his own seat belt in as he sees Danielle looking around. "Like the car?"

She nods.

"Good," he says before starting the car and moving it away from the curb. "So, I hope you like Italian food."

She nods again.

"Great, 'cause I'm taking you to the best Italian restaurant in town."

AS THE CAR comes to a stop, Danielle looks out the window in shock. They're in front of a grand hotel, and she guesses the restaurant is inside. She hears the door open and turns to watch Trevor stepping out of the car. She watches him close the door, jog around the car, and open her door. He smiles down at her and holds his hand out toward her. She takes her seat belt off and accepts his hand. He helps her out of the car and pushes the door closed before tossing his keys to a guy wearing a red vest and black pants, who Danielle assumes is a valet.

"Would you like it in your normal spot, sir?" asks the valet.

"Sure," Trevor answers and looks at Danielle, who raises her eyebrow. "I'll explain later."

Danielle nods her head. She's very confused. *Normal spot? He's been here before? Well, of course he has. But how many times?* She gazes around and notices the valets watching them with grins across their lips. Trevor greets them with handshakes.

Okay. What's going on?

They walk inside the hotel and are greeted by some of the

workers. Danielle's eyes wander around, and she is amazed at the lavish but comfortable interior. Trevor glances at her and smiles before leading her past the lobby and over toward a closed glass door. He pulls open the door, letting her walk in first.

Whoa ... this looks expensive.

Danielle gazes around, seeing the tables with white table-cloths, black leather chairs surrounding them, chandeliers hanging from the ceiling, and a fireplace on the other side of the room. She bites her lower lip, feeling like she's a little under dressed but she remembers Trevor's not wearing anything too fancy either.

"Ah, Mr. Williams." A middle-aged man dressed in a black suit and tie walks over to them and shakes Trevor's hand. "How many will be eating with you this evening?"

"Just the two of us," Trevor answers politely, "and anywhere will be fine."

"Very well. Follow me."

The man grabs two menus and starts walking away from them. Trevor lets go of Danielle's hand to rest his hand on her lower back as they follow him. They watch him put the menus on the table, and he pulls out a chair for Danielle. She smiles politely before sitting down.

"How's your father this evening?"

Trevor sits down across from Danielle. "Very well. Thank you."

"Well, I hope you enjoy your night and your waiter will be right with you."

"Thank you, Mr. Davidson," says Trevor.

The man walks away, and Danielle is now more puzzled than ever. She looks at Trevor with her right eyebrow raised. She wants to know how he knows that man so well. Or why the valets treated him the way they did and why they were greeted by all the workers.

Trevor can sense her looking at him, and he shifts in his seat. "Now, let's see what's good to eat, huh?"

He grabs the menu off the table and opens it. He looks at it, trying to avoid the questioning eyes of his date. He knows she has questions. Not able to avoid it anymore, he sighs and looks up to see her still staring at him, so he puts the menu down.

"Want answers?"

Danielle nods.

"Okay. My family owns this hotel-slash-resort and other hotels across the country," he explains. "This one is the Crystal Waves Hotel and Resort." He pauses. "I come here a lot. I'm next in line for the business, and I'm supposed to take over the family business when I graduate college. So, my family is kind of ... well-off."

Danielle's mouth opens in shock. She can't believe it. The guy she's slowly falling for and the guy she's been spending time with is rich—no, scratch that. He's wealthy. He never told her, and she wants to understand why. She reaches for her clutch to take out her phone.

Why didn't you tell me?

Trevor reads it and takes a breath. "I guess ... I didn't want you to know right away. I've had one or two girlfriends and friends who only liked me 'cause of the money and popularity. They didn't like me for me, and when I ran into you, I wanted you to. So ... I waited to see where things went."

Danielle smiles. That's a good enough answer for her. She reaches her hand across the table, lacing their hands together. He looks at her.

Using her other hand, she types.

I don't care about the money or the popularity. I'm not that kind of girl.
I wish you'd trusted me to tell me.

"I trust you. It's why I brought you here. I was going to wait a little longer to tell you, but I didn't want to hide this side of me from you." He gives her hand a slight squeeze. "And I hope that's okay. The food is excellent, but we can go somewhere else if you're uncomfortable."

She shakes her head as she pulls her hand away and picks up the menu. Trevor grins and picks up his own menu just as a waiter walks over to their table.

"Good evening, Mr. Williams," the young waiter says. "I'm Adam, and I'll be your waiter tonight. May I get you and your date something to drink?"

"Yes. And I think we're ready to order our meals too," Trevor says and looks up at him. "I will have a cola and the fettuccine with mussels marinara."

Trevor closes his menu and puts it on the table near the waiter. They both turn to Danielle, who looks at Trevor blankly before reaching for her phone. He inwardly groans at himself for forgetting she's not going to speak. As he's about to say something, she pushes her phone toward him. He looks at it and grins.

"She'll have the same as me but with a lemon-lime soda instead," he says. "Oh, and we'll share a sampler of every appetizer."

"Okay, great." The waiter picks up the menus. "I will be right back with your drinks."

After the waiter walks away, Trevor looks at Danielle with an apologetic look. "I kinda forgot about the no talking."

Danielle shakes her head with a smile, assuring him it's okay. He smiles, knowing she is different from all the other girls he's met. A good kind of different.

"Really don't care about the money?"

She shakes her head.

As long as your parents aren't like those in books and movies, where all they care about is money and fame.

Trevor laughs. "Don't worry. My parents aren't like that. They are down-to-earth. And I'm pretty sure if they weren't, my dad would probably have me take over the business now while going to college. So no worries; they aren't scary."

Danielle laughs and then gets curious.

Speaking of colleges, where are you going?

"Stanford," says Trevor after reading the phone, and he sits back against his chair, sighing. "It's kind of a family tradition to go there."

You don't sound thrilled about that idea.

Trevor shrugs his shoulders. "It's not that I don't want to go there. It's a great school. Don't get me wrong. But … it would be nice to choose my own school. I did, however, apply to other schools, but in the end, Stanford is the way to go in the Williams family."

Danielle moves her head up and down in understanding.

"How about you?" Trevor leans forward, resting his arms on the table.

She smiles while typing on her phone.

Harvard. It's where I've always wanted to go. My mom went there, and she always told me amazing stories about her experience there. And it just meant a lot to her … and me when I got accepted. It took our minds off her cancer for just a little bit.

Trevor smiles and reaches for her hand, lacing their fingers together. "Harvard is a great school. It actually was one of my other choices. They are lucky to have you."

Their eyes connect, and they sit in comfortable silence.

DANIELLE WIPES her mouth with a napkin and puts it down on the table. She sits back against the chair as she finishes her meal. She's in love with this place. Trevor is right about it being the best Italian restaurant in town. *Might be the best in the whole state.*

"We still have time."

She looks at Trevor.

"Want to go for a walk on the beach?"

She nods.

After a few minutes, Trevor receives the bill from the waiter. He places the cash in the server book and doesn't ask for change when handing the book back to the waiter. The waiter thanks them and wishes them a good rest of the evening.

Trevor stands up and walks over to Danielle. He pulls the chair back and holds his hand out. She grins as she takes his hand and then stands up. They lace their fingers together and walk out of the restaurant. She starts to walk to the right, but he starts pulling her to the left. She glances at him, confused, and he grins.

"We don't need the car."

She narrows her eyes at him and lets him pull her along. He leads her through the hotel, and once they reach the back, he pushes through a door. They walk outside, and Danielle's eyes widen as she notices the sand. She looks at Trevor.

"I forgot to mention that this hotel is right on the beach," he says and turns to her. "Ready to take that walk?"

She nods but holds her finger up and removes her hand from his. He looks at her with one eyebrow raised until she rests her hand on his shoulder. He watches her bend her leg up behind her, so she can remove her left heel, and then she does the same with her right heel. Trevor holds his left hand out to take them, but she shakes her head and holds them in her right hand. She loops her arm with his. He can't stop the grin that forms on his lips. She looks at him and smiles softly before they take their first steps along the sand.

THE TWO CONTINUE quietly walking along the beach. It seems they are the only ones there, and it is nice. Danielle looks over to her right and smiles, seeing the light of the moon shining down onto the water. *It's so peaceful.*

Trevor looks down at her and can't help but smile, seeing her eyes light up at the sight.

"So … enjoying the beach?"

She looks at him and nods.

"Me too," he says, "especially at night when the stars and moon are shining down. And definitely when I get to walk along it with a pretty girl like you."

Danielle blushes. He grins and slides her hand off his arm, so he can take it in his hand. He intertwines their fingers together. She lowers her eyes down at their hands and can't help but notice how perfectly their hands fit together. Butterflies fill her stomach.

Tonight can't get any better.

A breeze goes across Danielle's body, and she shivers. Trevor notices and lets go of her hand. He pushes his jacket off his shoulders and throws it around her. He turns toward her, so he can pull it forward and moves her hair, letting it lie on the jacket. She stares at him as his hands slide down the jacket, and he holds it near the opening by her waist. Their eyes connect, and he pulls on the jacket to bring her closer to him.

"You have beautiful eyes."

Danielle blushes, and she bites her lower lip. Trevor moves his right hand up to move a strand of hair to behind her ear. Then, he rests his hand on her face and caresses her cheek with his thumb. He puts his other hand under the jacket and rests it on her waist. He lowers his eyes to her lips and then moves them back up before closing his eyes. He leans in, and Danielle stops biting her lip as she closes her eyes. As their lips touch, she drops her heels and wraps her arms around his neck. He moves his hand away from her cheek and down to her waist.

Trevor pulls back when air is needed and opens his eyes to stare at Danielle as her eyes flutter open. He moves his hands to her lower back and caresses her with his thumbs as their eyes stay connected.

"Elle," Trevor says, "I hope it's okay I call you that."

She nods.

"Good," says Trevor. "I know this is only our first date, but I've enjoyed the time we've spent together. Will you be my girlfriend?"

She grins before leaning up to press her lips against his for a soft, gentle kiss, and then she pulls back, still grinning.

"I will take that as a yes."

She laughs and nods.

AT TEN THIRTY P.M., Trevor and Danielle walk up the stairs of Grandma Marie's front porch. They know she said that they could stay out later, but Trevor wants to stay on her good side, so he's brought Danielle home at a decent time.

"I had a great time tonight." He turns to Danielle. "Best first date."

Danielle nods in agreement. She smiles as she shrugs the jacket off her shoulders and hands it to him before turning toward the front door. Trevor chuckles as he reaches his hand out to grab hers before she can open the door. He turns her around and pulls her close to him. He rests his hand on her waist as he leans in and captures her lips with his own.

He pulls back and presses his forehead against hers. "Good night."

Trevor smiles. He slowly backs up away from her. She opens her eyes to watch him walk down the stairs and over to his car. He opens the driver's door, steps into the car, and puts his seat belt on. He looks back at Danielle and waves. She grins as she waves back before turning around and walking into the house. She closes the door and leans her back against it as she grins.

"Nice night?" Grandma Marie asks as she smiles at her granddaughter.

Danielle doesn't make any movement as she stays in a trance.

"I'm guessing it was." Grandma Marie laughs. "Oh … your dad called."

Danielle looks at her grandma.

"He said he was sorry for not calling when he got home the other day," says Grandma Marie, "and that he loves you and hopes you're doing okay."

Danielle sighs, knowing he cares and wants her to talk soon but she's not ready yet. She knows what will get her talking again, but that might be awhile. She wants her next words to be *I love you* because those were the last ones she said. She could easily say them to Jacob, her dad, or her grandma, but it would be too easy. For those words to come out, they have to be for someone else, and it scares her that she already believes Trevor could be that someone. She bites her lower lip, knowing she's never felt like this for anyone before.

6

THE BIRD'S NEST

*J*acob walks around the backyard, bored and looking for something to do. He looks up at the tree and notices something sitting on one branch. He wants to see what it is. He sees how high the tree is and pouts as he remembers he's not allowed to climb trees without anyone's supervision. He turns around and runs into the house, looking for Danielle.

Going in the living room, he finds her sitting on the couch, reading a magazine. "Dani?"

She looks up from her magazine.

"There's something in the tree, and I really, really want to know what it is."

Danielle throws the magazine onto the couch before pushing herself up. She walks over to Jacob, grabbing his hand. She has an idea what it is but isn't too sure. Jacob walks with Danielle out of the house and over to the tree. He points up to the branch.

"Can you climb up with me?"

Danielle sighs and looks up at the tree. She usually doesn't like climbing up trees and was never planning on climbing this one, as it's one of the highest trees she's ever seen. She looks down at

Jacob, seeing that he desperately wants to go up. She bites her lower lip but comes up with an idea. She reaches inside her pocket to take her phone out.

Danielle: *Hey. Could u come over? Jacob wants to climb up the tree in our yard to see what's up there, and I hate climbing trees. It's probably just a bird's nest, but ... he really wants to go up.*

Jacob watches Danielle with confusion as he wonders why she's on her phone but shrugs it off, knowing she's going to find some way for him to go up.

Danielle feels her phone vibrating and then looks at it.

Trevor: *Sure. I'll be there in five.*

She smiles, and she slides her phone back into her pocket. She looks at Jacob and holds up her hand, meaning five minutes. He groans and crosses his arms but stops when Danielle gives him a stern look. He uncrosses his arms and nods.

"Right ... five minutes."

TREVOR PUSHES the outside gate open and walks into the backyard. He looks over to see Jacob sitting on the ground while his girl-friend lies on the ground with her eyes closed. He smirks as he walks over to her and stands right above her to block the sun. Danielle groans as she opens her eyes and glares up at him.

"Sorry if I ruined whatever you were doing." He laughs as he reaches his hand out. "But I believe someone and I have some climbing to do."

"Finally," Jacob says as he jumps up from the ground, but Danielle stares at him sternly as she stands up with help from Trevor. "I mean … thank you."

Jacob puts his two thumbs up, and Danielle rolls her eyes. Trevor smiles at them, loving how close they are to each other. No matter what the age difference is, they are as close as they could be. Makes him wish he had a sibling. Danielle looks over at Trevor and motions her head at the tree. He nods and walks over to it with Jacob next to him.

"Have you ever climbed a tree before?"

Jacob shakes his head. "I was never allowed."

"All right!" Trevor claps his hands together. "I'm going to help you get up there. It's much easier than it looks, and I'll be with you every step."

While Trevor explains and shows the way to climb the tree, Danielle drags one of the lounge chairs over to the grass and turns it to face the tree before sitting down. She looks over to watch the two start their climb.

"It doesn't seem that hard," says Jacob as he sets himself up onto the trunk.

"I told you it wasn't." Trevor laughs as he climbs up. "All you have to do is take it slow, and before you know it, you'll be at the branch you want to be at."

After a few more pull-ups and help from Trevor, Jacob reaches the branch. Trevor tells him to hold on as he goes to settle himself on one of the nearby stable branches. He reaches his hand down for Jacob to grab and pulls him up to sit on the same branch. Trevor keeps a hand on him, and he puts his other hand on the tree trunk as he looks down to see Danielle smiling.

"I did it!" Jacob exclaims.

Danielle puts her thumb up in the air. Trevor looks over at the other branch across from them and sees that she was right about it being a bird's nest. It has tiny eggs lying in it. He taps Jacob's leg and points it out to him.

"What is that?"

"That's a bird's nest," Trevor says but sees he's puzzled. "It's where a mommy bird lays her babies in. Before they become baby birds, they are in eggs. Then, they hatch and are born."

"That's so cool!" Jacob is amused at the sight and carefully leans forward. "But where is the mommy bird? Is she going to be back when they hatch?"

"It is unusual, seeing a bird's nest without a mommy or daddy bird protecting the eggs, but maybe they are getting ready to hatch and went to get them some food."

"I hope they come back in time, so the babies don't die."

"I'll tell you what." Jacob looks back at Trevor. "I'll come here every day to check up on them and see if they've hatched yet. If they do and neither mommy nor daddy birds are back, I'll call the Humane Society, and they will come to make sure they get what they need, okay?"

"I'd like that." Jacob nods his head. "And you can spend more time with my sister."

"Yeah, but also with you too, little man."

"Okay," Jacob says. "I guess we have to go back down now?"

Trevor nods his head.

"Okay."

Trevor removes his arm from Jacob and helps him get into the position he needs to be in for him to climb back down. But before he starts, Trevor goes down first, so he can keep a better eye on him in case something happens. They start making their way down. Once Trevor touches the ground, he holds his hands out to support Jacob before he jumps down to the ground. They give each other a high five. Jacob excitedly runs over to Danielle.

"It's a bird's nest with eggs in it! But the mommy and daddy birds aren't there," Jacob starts as Trevor sits down in one of the other lounge chairs. "So, Trevor said he would come over to watch them, and if they hatch without the mommy and daddy birds, he will call the Humane Society to have them take care of them."

Danielle nods and giggles at her brother's enthusiasm. She moves her eyes to Trevor, who winks at her, before looking back at Jacob, who rambles on about the bird's nest.

"I'm going to go tell Grandma!" He runs into the house.

"Wow. I've never seen a little kid get that excited unless it's Christmas morning." Trevor laughs as he watches Jacob and then looks at Danielle. "So ... you don't like climbing trees?"

She shakes her head.

"Did something happen or just don't like it?"

She nods.

He laughs. "Which one is it?"

She puts up her pointer finger meaning the first one.

"Ah. Okay, I get it," he says. "Want to head inside or hang out here?"

She leans back against the chair. He nods but gets up, so he can pull his chair next to hers before sitting back down. He reaches his hand over to grab hers, lacing their fingers together, and lays his head against his chair. She looks over at him, grinning, and shifts closer to him, resting her head on his shoulder. She closes her eyes.

7

NEW JOB

*D*anielle sits on the edge of her bed, waiting for the doorbell to ring. Their dad is coming to visit, and she's confused about it since he said they wouldn't see him until the end of summer. He must have something to tell them, and she hopes it's a good something, but she has a weird feeling in her stomach.

"Daddy's here!"

Jacob runs into Danielle's bedroom and grabs her hand, pulling her off the bed. He pulls her with him down the stairs just as the front door opens. John walks in, grinning. He kisses his mom's cheek and then walks over to his kids.

"Well, if it isn't the two greatest kids in the world," he says as he hugs each of them.

"Daddy!" Jacob returns the hug before pulling back. "Why are you here?"

"I wanted to see how everyone was doing. But I also have something important to tell you," he says. "We should go into the living room."

They walk into the room. Danielle and Jacob sit down on one couch while Grandma Marie sits on the other couch, which is on the opposite side of the coffee table. As John sits next to his mom, he's nervous about the news he has to tell them. He doesn't have any idea how they will take it but understands they have to know. He takes a deep breath.

Grandma Marie looks at him. "John … what's wrong?"

"I'll come right out and say it," he says as he puts his hands together. "I lost my job."

Danielle looks at him in shock. She'd be screaming if she was talking. *What are we supposed to do now? If he doesn't have a job, how are we supposed to live? Or how will Harvard get paid for?*

John can read Danielle's worrisome facial expression. "But I'm going to find a new job. There is nothing to worry about."

She shakes her head. She knows it will take her dad time to find a job. Probably months. Like last time, when he got laid off from his previous job, a few years ago. She knows they have money in savings, as she's good with numbers and she always helped her parents with their money. But it still isn't enough. She can't take sitting there, so she stands up before running out.

John gets ready to stand up. "I'll go talk to her."

"Don't. Let her be," Grandma Marie says. "She needs time."

He sighs and sits back against the couch. Grandma Marie pats his shoulder. Neither notices Jacob getting up from the couch and walking out of the room. Grabbing the phone off the kitchen counter, he dials a familiar number.

"Can you come over?" he asks once the person answers. "My daddy lost his job, and Dani ran upstairs."

"Sure. I'll be right over," the voice says before hanging up.

JACOB SITS ON THE COUCH. impatiently waiting. He looks over at his dad, who keeps looking from the floor to the hallway, hoping Danielle will come back down the stairs. The doorbell rings. Grandma Marie gets ready to stand up but stops when Jacob jumps up from the couch and runs out of the living room. John looks at his mom, perplexed, and she shrugs her shoulders.

Jacob opens the door to let the person in.

"Where is she?"

John walks over. "Who's this?"

"This is Trevor, my buddy and Danielle's boyfriend."

"Boyfriend?" John stands there, taken aback, as he's never heard of him before. "Well … it's nice to meet you."

"It's nice to meet you too, sir," Trevor says as he puts his hand out. "I'm sorry for the loss of your wife."

"Thank you," John says as he shakes his hand, already liking him. "Dani's up in her room. You can go see her."

"Thanks," Trevor says before running up the stairs. He walks down the hall, looking for her door before knocking on it. "Elle, it's me. Can I come in?"

The door slowly opens. He looks at her and can see she's been crying. He reaches his arms out and pulls her into his chest as he rubs her back. She cries into his arms, and he carefully pushes her into the room without letting her go before kicking the door closed. They walk over to her bed and sit down on the edge of it. Trevor lets her go, so he can slide up onto the bed and lie on it. He opens his arms for Danielle to lie down with him.

"Shh … what happened?"

Danielle wipes her eyes before reaching over to grab her phone.

My dad lost his job, just when we really needed the money. He needs

to take care of Jacob and pay for Harvard. I have scholarships, but it
still won't be enough.
It'll take him months to get a new job.

He reads it and nods in understanding. He kisses the top of her
head, knowing how important going to Harvard is to her. It's
something she shared with her mom. He shifts a little, so he can
reach his hand into his pocket. Taking his phone out, he dials a
number.

"Dad?" Trevor asks into the phone. He explains the situation.
"Please, Dad. I'll never ask you for something this big again ...
Thank you ... I'll see you later ... Yeah, yeah. Bye."

He presses the End button and throws the phone on the bed.
Then, he looks down at Danielle, who stares up at him with confusion in her bloodshot eyes. "I got your dad a job."

She mouths, *How?*

"I talked to my dad about giving him a job at one of our hotels.
It's a few miles away from the one we went to on our first date."

Danielle opens her mouth in shock.

"I get how important Jacob and Harvard are to you, so I wanted
to do this one thing for your family," he says as he wipes away a
tear that fell from her eye. "Plus, your dad shouldn't have to take
money out of his savings. Not yet."

She grins and wraps her arms around his torso, hugging him.
She pulls back and looks up to press her lips to his for a slow
thank-you kiss. Then, she pulls away before sitting up and jumping
up off the bed. She grabs Trevor's hand, making him get up with
her, and they run out of her room, down the stairs, and into the
living room.

"Whoa, what's with the rush?" John asks.

Danielle looks at Trevor, nudging him. Trevor chuckles, understanding why she dragged him all the way down the stairs, almost causing him to fall.

"I think Elle wants me to tell you about the job I got for you."

John raises his eyebrow. "Job? What job?"

"My family owns a chain of hotels, and I called my dad. Told him about your situation, and he said that there's an opening at one hotel that's about ten to fifteen miles away from here."

"I can't have you do that, son." He shakes his head. "I should be able to find my own job."

"I understand, but I also know how important Harvard was to Danielle and her mom," Trevor says as he squeezes Danielle's hand, "and I don't think you should have to take money from your savings to make payments when you have to take care of Jacob too. It was either the job or I'd find some way to help pay for Harvard too."

Danielle's mouth opens wide as she gazes at him. She would not let him do that, but she also knows he probably wouldn't take no for an answer. She closes her mouth and looks over at her dad, nodding her head. John looks around the room—from his mom to Jacob to Trevor and to Danielle, who he knows wants to go to Harvard for her mom.

He smiles as he stands up before walking over to them, and he puts his hand out.

"I'll take it."

"Great! You definitely won't regret this, sir," says Trevor while shaking his hand. "Welcome to the hotel business."

"Thank you," says John before nodding at Danielle. "He's a good one."

Danielle grins as she looks at Trevor, agreeing with her dad.

Yeah ... he is. I'm definitely slowly falling in love with him. It's still too soon, but I am. And it doesn't scare me as much as it did before.

8

MEETING THE PARENTS

"*E*lle?" Trevor looks over at her as she's sitting on one of the lounge chairs in the backyard. "I was wondering if you and your family would like to come over to my house and have dinner with me"—he pauses—"and my parents."

Danielle sits up in her seat and looks at him, surprised. She isn't sure what to say or think. *How am I supposed to meet his parents when I'm not speaking?* Trevor can tell she's worried and freaking out inside; it's like he can read her mind.

"Don't worry. They know about the no-talking thing, and they don't care," he says and grabs her hand. "They want to meet you. And I want you to meet them."

She bites her lower lip before nodding her head. He grins and kisses the back of her hand.

"They're going to love you," he says. "I know they will."

"Are you ready to meet his parents?" John glances at Danielle, who stares blankly at the dark blue door. "Hey, it's going to be okay. I remember being nervous when I met your grandparents, but they made me comfortable and welcomed me with opened arms."

Danielle looks at him and smiles. She knows their story. Her parents met in the summer, like she and Trevor did. They fell in love and were married until her mom passed away. They spent twenty years together. She knows they loved each other. She wants that. She wants the same relationship her parents had, if that's even possible.

"Come on. I'm hungry," Jacob says impatiently and knocks on the door.

The door opens a few moments later, and a young woman with wavy red hair stands there with a smile. They look at her, and Danielle believes this woman could be someone who works for Trevor's family, as there isn't any resemblance between them.

"Hi! You must be the Washingtons," she says with enthusiasm. "Come on in. The Williams are in the living room, so you're welcome to walk right in."

Grandma Marie says, "Thank you."

Before anyone can make their way in, Jacob runs in first. No one tries to stop him, knowing there isn't any point in doing so.

"Trevor …" Jacob abruptly stops at the living room doorway as he sees a man sitting on the couch with a woman. "Um … hi."

They smile at him and stand up from the couch. He nervously bites his lower lip as they walk over to him. He doesn't recognize them, and he's worried about what they're going to do, but that all stops when he hears Trevor's voice behind him.

"Hey, little man."

Jacob turns around to see Trevor holding Danielle's hand.

"Mom, Dad, this is Jacob, Danielle's little brother, and this"— Trevor pushes Danielle slightly forward—"is Danielle, my girlfriend."

The woman grins as she walks over to Danielle and wraps her arms around her. "It's so nice to meet you. Trevor never stops talking about you."

Danielle smiles as she accepts the hug and giggles when she hears Trevor groaning behind them, embarrassed at his mom's comment. She pulls back.

"Danielle"—the man next to her puts his hand out—"it's very nice to meet you. I'm Joe, and this crazy hugging woman"—he chuckles while motioning his head to the woman—"is Sarah."

She laughs as she shakes Joe's hand. Joe and Sarah introduce themselves to John and Marie while Trevor and Danielle walk into the living room. They sit on the couch. Jacob follows them but sits on the floor in front of the couch.

"Your house is huge," Jacob says as he looks around. "I can't wait to be your brother!"

Danielle's eyes widen, and she kicks him lightly.

He falls over and then sits up, glaring at her as he crosses his arms. "Well, sorry."

"Ah, Jacob, you're already like my brother, so don't worry about your sister." Trevor laughs as he leans forward to high-five him. "We'll work on her."

Danielle shakes her head and laughs. She likes the fact that one of the most important people in her life loves the new guy in her life. She always worried about when she had a boyfriend, if Jacob would like him or not. If her boyfriend didn't get along with him, then they wouldn't be dating for long.

"I've never seen him like this before," says Sarah after seeing his interaction with Jacob.

"Your son is a great kid," Grandma Marie says. "A few days ago, he came to our house to climb a tree with Jacob, so he could see what was in the tree."

"He told us about that," says Sarah.

John looks at Joe and asks, "What kind of work will I be doing?"

"Well … we need a new manager to run the day-to-day operations at one of our hotels," Joe says as they each sit down in a chair. "Trevor explained your situation, and since Danielle means a lot to my son and to you, I want to help. I can already tell you will be the perfect person for the job."

"Manager?" John stares at him in shock. "Are you sure?"

"I looked into you and heard you used to be a manager at your previous job, but you were laid off because you were having a difficult time focusing since your wife passed, which I'm very sorry to hear about," says Joe. "But I think you're still right for this position."

John looks over at Danielle. She's laughing with Trevor and Jacob. He can tell she's healing from her mom's death, and it's time for him to do the same. They will always love her, and she would want them to move on. He takes a deep breath and looks at Joe.

"I would love to take the job."

"Great," Joe says as he claps his hands together and sits straight up in his chair. "Oh, and Danielle's first payment to Harvard will be taken care of."

"Oh, no, no." John shakes his head. "The job is enough. I could never ask you to do that."

"I'm not asking. I'm telling." Joe shrugs his shoulders and motions his head at Trevor. "He has never felt this way about someone before. She must be special, and I want to help in any way I can."

"As long as I can pay you back."

"There's no need. Harvard is expensive, and you have Jacob to take care of."

John sighs, knowing he won't win. "Okay. And thank you."

∼

DANIELLE WIPES her mouth with her napkin and rests it on the table next to her plate as she looks around the table, realizing she was worried about nothing. Everyone is getting along great. She looks down and smiles to herself, not noticing Trevor staring at her. He realizes something in that moment. She's the *one*. He's in love with her, but he wants to take it slow, so he doesn't scare her away. Danielle looks up at him, and she blushes.

Trevor winks and turns to his mom. "The dinner was great, Mom."

"Thanks, sweetie." She gives him a proud smile. "I hope everyone liked it?"

She looks around the table as everyone nods their heads. Joe looks at her and grins, knowing it thrills her that the food came out good. And it did. Sarah did all the cooking that evening, which is something she doesn't always do. They sometimes hire a cook, but tonight was a special night for Trevor, so Sarah cooked.

"Now, while we adults move into the living room for some drinks, you kids can go do whatever you want," Joe says as he stands up.

John, Grandma Marie, and Sarah stand. Sarah tells them not to worry about the plates, as they will clean up later. The four adults walk out of the dining room. Jacob sighs and rests his head against his arm that's lying on the table. Trevor looks at him and can sense that he's bored.

"Hey, buddy, want to go to the game room and play some games?"

"Yeah!" Jacob jumps up from the chair and looks at Trevor. "Are you going to play too?"

Trevor glances at Danielle, knowing he wants to spend some

time with her tonight, but stands from his chair as he looks at Jacob. "I'll play a couple. Let's go."

Danielle stands up and follows the two. They walk out of the dining room, turn to their left, and head up the stairs and down the hallway, passing a few doors before Trevor pushes one open. He walks in, followed by Danielle. Jacob runs in but stops as he gazes around with his mouth wide open, noticing the enormous room full of arcade games.

"Cool, huh?"

"Yes!"

Trevor chuckles. He puts his hands on Jacob's shoulders and pushes him toward a Whack-A-Mole game. Danielle watches them before she walks around the room, looking for a game she can play by herself. She stops when she sees it—her favorite game in the entire world—and she can't hide her excitement because she hasn't played it in a long time. She walks up to it and smiles when she stares up at the name.

Dance Dance Revolution, the all-time greatest game ever. Still sucks they closed down the arcade back home. I've missed this game.

She grins as she slides her sweater off her shoulders, leaving her in a blue tank top, and rests it on the chair next to the game. She steps up onto the stage and stretches. She reaches forward to press the Start button, and her feet start following the lit dance steps on the floor.

Trevor hears the music and stops whacking for a moment as he looks around until he sees Danielle dancing with an enormous smile. His eyes widen in amazement at how good she is. Just when he thought she couldn't be any more perfect, she proves him wrong.

Jacob stops whacking, confused, until he sees where Trevor is looking and exclaims, "Oh! You have Dance Dance Revolution!"

"Yeah." Trevor looks down at Jacob. "Why?"

"That was the most popular game back home. But the arcade closed down, and we couldn't find another," Jacob explains. "Dani used to be the best in town. Not even the girls on the dance team could beat her."

"Oh, really?"

Jacob nods his head, and Trevor looks over at Danielle.

"Well, it so happens that I'm the champ in this town, so we'll see who is the best."

Trevor rests the foam hammer on the game before he makes his way over to Dance Dance Revolution. Knowing he's going to get hot, he pulls his shirt over his head and rests it on top of Danielle's sweater. He steps up onto the stage and presses the Stop button. Danielle raises her eyebrow and looks at him, but then she lowers her eyes when she realizes he's shirtless. She can't take her eyes off his muscular, tan body.

"Like what you see?" Trevor smirks as she continues to stare at him. "All right, are you going to stare, or you want to see if you can beat the real champ?"

Danielle smirks and shakes her head. She playfully pushes him before starting the game. She giggles as she moves her feet along with the lights.

"Okay, two can play that game," he says as he steadies himself. He moves his feet with the lights, but out of nowhere, he pokes Danielle. "Oops."

But Danielle expected that, so instead of losing her balance, she holds on to the bar behind her and steadies herself quicker than Trevor does. They both continue to follow the steps as they laugh with one another, having fun. Danielle is winning. But Trevor isn't giving up that easily. Glancing behind them to make sure Jacob isn't watching, he reaches over and grabs Danielle's hand, and he pulls her toward him. He leans down and presses his lips to hers, giving her a passionate kiss while the game's music continues. She moans against his lips.

He pulls back with a smirk. "Let's see if you can focus now."

He continues to smirk as he turns and goes right back to dancing. Danielle looks at him in a daze but shakes her head. She changes her facial expression to a shocked one. But she comes up with a plan. She looks back to see Jacob is now watching them, and she winks at him. Jacob puts his thumb up, knowing what to do.

Danielle turns away and watches Trevor. She decides not to go back to dancing right away, letting him think he's going to win but he's so very wrong.

Jacob runs around the room and then crashes into one of the games. "Ow!"

He pretends to cry. Danielle widens her eyes but isn't worried. Trevor stops dancing and jumps off the stage, running over to help Jacob. While focusing on Jacob, he doesn't notice Danielle laughing as she starts dancing again. She ends up beating him.

Jacob stops crying and looks up at him while laughing. "You just lost!"

"What?" Trevor stands back, perplexed, but senses Danielle standing behind him. Then, he looks at the game's screen to see Danielle's name with *Winner* flashing above it. "Oh … you two are good."

"We know." Jacob grins as he jumps up and high-fives Danielle. "It always works."

Trevor laughs as he shakes his head. He can't believe he fell for it and lost the game.

"I totally knew that wasn't real," he says.

Danielle and Jacob stare at each other with their eyebrows

raised and then look back at Trevor, shaking their heads. Trevor chuckles, knowing he got beat.

He saunters over to Danielle and rests his hands on her waist.

"Ya know ... you weren't that bad."

Danielle grins and nods her head while wrapping her arms around his neck. They both stare at each other. Trevor leans in but is interrupted.

"Hey. There's a kid in the room." Jacob crosses his arms.

"Sorry, little man." Trevor releases his arms and puts a hand on Jacob's shoulder, turning him around to face the other way. "Is that better?"

"Whatever. I'm going to go play a game." Jacob grunts as he stomps over to a game.

Trevor laughs as he turns back to Danielle. "Ya know I'm still not wearing a shirt, right?"

She lowers her eyes, looking at his shirtless, muscular, tan body. She bites her lower lip as she looks back up nodding. He grins as he places one of his hands back on her waist and moves his other hand to her cheek, caressing it with his thumb. She closes her eyes, leaning into his hand as she rests her hands against his chest. Trevor smiles. He closes his eyes and leans in to capture Danielle's lips with his. She smiles against his lips as she returns the kiss.

Trevor slides his hand down to her waist to pull her closer to him as they deepen the kiss. Danielle slides her own hands up his chest and to the back of his head. He groans as their bodies touch each other. As he's about to open his mouth, they get interrupted by someone clearing their throat. They pull back from each other and look over by the door to see their parents and Grandma Marie looking at them.

"Um, hi," Trevor says with a squeak in his voice and then looks down, remembering he isn't wearing a shirt. He steps away from

Danielle. "This isn't what it looks like. I took my shirt off to play Dance Dance Revolution, so I wouldn't get it too wet with sweat because that game can really get you sweaty and—"

"Trevor," Joe says, "we know. We were watching. I'm glad someone beat you."

"Wow, Dad. Thanks." He rolls his eyes. "Wait … you were watching? The whole time?"

Sarah says, "Just for the past few minutes."

Danielle's cheeks turn red in embarrassment because they were watching them. They saw them making out. Trevor notices the scared expression on her face and grabs her hand, pulling her close to him.

"Okay … can you please leave?" asks Trevor. "You're making us a little uncomfortable."

"Right, sorry. We will leave you three alone," John says and then looks at his daughter. "We'll be leaving in about an hour."

Danielle nods her head in agreement. The four adults turn and leave the room. Trevor and Danielle take a deep breath before looking at each other.

"Well, that was embarrassing," Trevor says, "but the kiss was amazing."

She blushes and points to his shirt.

"Right, okay." He kisses her cheek before walking over to pick up his shirt and put it on.

EVERYONE STANDS near the door as Danielle, Jacob, John, and Grandma Marie are getting ready to leave. Trevor doesn't want them to leave yet but knows they have to.

"I'll text ya later," he says as he gives Danielle a kiss. He looks at Jacob. "Later, buddy."

"Bye. Your house was so much fun!" Jacob exclaims. "Can I come back?"

"Of course. You are all welcome to come back whenever you want," Sarah says. "Our door is always open to you."

"Thank you for a lovely evening." Marie shakes Joe's hand and then Sarah's, as does John.

Trevor gives Danielle another kiss on her lips before opening the door and watching the Washingtons walk out of the house. Danielle smiles as they head down the steps.

The night ended up being a success. She was nervous for nothing and knows she won't have to be nervous again. Trevor was right. His parents are down-to-earth.

"See, you had nothing to worry about," John says.

She nods her head as she thinks back on the night and Trevor. She learned something about herself that night. She's in love. But she doesn't want to scare him away, and she's not ready to talk or say the words *I love you* yet. They're still young. It's too early in their relationship for those three important words. Maybe one day.

9

HATCHING

*E*ver since Trevor showed Jacob the nest in the tree, he runs outside to check on it to see if the mommy or daddy bird has returned, and so far, they haven't. Trevor has told him that the eggs should be getting ready to hatch soon, and Jacob is worried.

"How are the eggs today?" Trevor asks as he stands on the porch, looking at Jacob.

"They haven't hatched yet," Jacob says as he turns to Trevor, "and the mommy or daddy bird hasn't come back yet."

Danielle walks out the back door and stands next to Trevor as she looks up at the tree. She's worried too. Their family loves animals, and they want to help every animal, no matter how dangerous it is. They did it last year with Bobcat, the turtle.

"It'll be okay," Trevor says, reassuring him. "I already called the Humane Society, and they said they'll come right away after the eggs hatch."

"I hope you're right."

Trevor smiles before staring up at the tree, and his right eyebrow goes up as he sees something moving. He gets curious and trudges up to the tree. Danielle follows him but stops to stand next to Jacob. They stand there, puzzled, as they watch Trevor climb up the tree.

Jacob asks, "What are you doing?"

Trevor looks down and puts his finger to his mouth before he continues to climb taking branch by branch. He sees more movement coming from the nest. He climbs up one more branch before sitting on the strongest one, the same one he and Jacob sat on last time.

"Hey," he whispers as he looks down. "Jacob, climb up but do it slowly and quietly."

Jacob nods. He walks closer to the tree and starts to climb up, remembering how Trevor taught him. Danielle watches him closely in case he falls, but once he reaches the top, she smiles, as she has an idea of what's happening. Jacob gets settled on the branch with Trevor. He looks into the nest to notice the eggs moving.

"What's happening?"

Trevor answers, "The eggs are hatching."

"But the mommy and daddy birds aren't back yet."

"I know." Trevor looks down at Danielle. "Elle, can you call the Humane Society?"

Danielle raises her left eyebrow and crosses her arms. She points to her mouth and gives him a *how* expression. He nods his head, realizing she isn't able to.

"Right." He chuckles. "Can you go tell your grandma to call them or your cousin?"

She raises her right hand up to her forehead, saluting him. He laughs as she turns around, marching into the house to find Grandma Marie sitting at the kitchen table. She takes out her phone, and she types explaining what is happening. She hands it over. Grandma Marie reads it and stands up right away, walking over to grab her phone.

TREVOR AND JACOB are standing on the ground with everyone else as they stare up at the tree, watching the Humane Society guys carefully remove the nest. They waited a couple hours before doing so to make sure the parent birds were not hiding somewhere. The two men place the nest into a box for it to stay warm. Then, they climb down the tree. Once down, they show the box to those who are waiting. The four baby birds are chirping away.

John asks, "What's going to happen to them?"

"We will take excellent care of them. Then, when they are strong and healthy"—one man smiles—"we'll either set them free or put them in a zoo that takes donations, so they will be looked after. Just like Bobcat."

"I like the second choice," Jacob speaks up.

"All right, little man, we'll see what we can do," Keegan says as he rests his hand on Jacob's shoulder. "Well, we should get these babies to a safe environment."

Keegan gives everyone a hug before leaving with his fellow volunteers. Jacob smiles happily, knowing he saved more animals this year. Danielle giggles. She knows how happy he is and remembers his reaction when they found Bobcat last year. This is what she wants to do. She wants to help wildlife, and by the looks of it, Jacob wants to do the same thing.

John says, "Another happily ever after."

"We are good!" Jacob exclaims as he dances. "We need to do more, like now!"

"Whoa, Jacob." John laughs. "Saving an animal a year is a good start and is helping the world. So, you are doing a great job already."

"Fine," Jacob sighs as he walks in the house.

Danielle looks at her dad, shaking her head and giggling. He nods his head, knowing what she's thinking, and he jogs after Jacob. She sighs happily, knowing they helped a few more animals, and can tell this summer will end up being a great summer even though her mom isn't with them. She smiles when she sees Trevor lying on the ground with his eyes closed. But maybe … just maybe, her mom is the one who sent *him* to her.

10

EX-GIRLFRIEND

*D*anielle shifts her feet side to side through the white sand. She closes her eyes before she reopens them and starts walking on the beach. Still feeling good about the outcome of the baby birds, she's treating herself to a day of walking on the beach. She loves the beach. Besides it being peaceful, it was also her mom's favorite place to go, and she feels closer to her mom when she walks on the sand.

An arm snakes around her waist, and she looks to her right to see Trevor.

"You weren't thinking about taking a walk on the beach without me, were you?" He chuckles as he pulls her to his side.

Danielle giggles and shrugs her shoulders before leaning into his body. She was hoping to have the day to herself, but she always enjoys his company, so she doesn't mind.

TREVOR STOPS WALKING as he sees a girl with long black hair ahead of them. "Bianca?"

The girl turns around and grins. "Oh my God! Trevor ... hi!"

"Wow." Trevor takes his arm from Danielle and walks forward to hug the girl. "What are you doing here? I thought you weren't coming back this summer."

"Neither did I." She pulls back, grinning. "But we decided to come back before, ya know, college starts. The last hurrah, my dad calls it." She laughs. "I can't believe you're still here."

"I have nowhere to go." He shrugs his shoulders and laughs. "You look the same."

"So do you," she says as she twirls her hair with her pointer finger and looks him up and down with a glint in her eye. "Still the same hottie you always were."

Danielle bites her lower lip as she awkwardly stands to the side, slightly jealous when this girl, who she doesn't know, flirts with her boyfriend like that. But she knows Trevor wouldn't do anything to hurt her. She turns away to gaze out at the ocean.

She looks up at the sky, and she sees her mom looking down at her. Her eyes widen, but it disappears. She shakes her head, as she doesn't want it to go even though she knows it was her imagination. She looks back out to the water, and a tear falls down her cheek.

"Hey," Bianca says as she motions toward Danielle, "is she okay?"

Trevor looks over and sees the tear falling down Danielle's cheek. His heart breaks, and he walks over to her, wrapping his arms around her, pulling her to his chest.

"Elle, what's wrong?"

Danielle shakes her head against his chest and stays quiet. He pulls back and looks down at her, feeling concerned as he rubs her back.

"Shh ... whatever it is," he whispers, "I got you."

She pulls back and reaches into her pocket to take her phone out.

While you were talking to that girl, I thought I saw my mom's face in the sky, but it disappeared.

Trevor reads it and presses his lips to her forehead. "It'll be okay."

Bianca watches them with one eyebrow raised. *Who is she? Is he dating her? Why doesn't she talk? What's with using her phone?* She wipes her hands against her pants.

"Uh … Trevor?"

He looks behind them without letting go of Danielle and asks, "Yeah?"

"I'm gonna go," she says as she takes steps backward. "I'll, uh, see you later."

"No, wait. I want to introduce you to someone," he says as he moves his hands to wipe Danielle's tears away and turns them toward Bianca. "Bianca, this is Danielle, my girlfriend. Elle, this is Bianca. We went out last year."

Bianca reaches her hand out. "It's nice to meet you."

Danielle smiles as she shakes her hand. Bianca takes her hand back, confused.

"She doesn't talk," Trevor explains as he puts his arm around Danielle's waist. "She had a lot happen before the summer started."

"Oh." Bianca nods. "Well … I should go … I hope I see you again … Danielle."

Danielle nods.

"Well, bye," says Bianca before she turns around and hurries off.

Trevor turns to Danielle and sees she still has some tears in her eyes. He leans down and kisses her eyelids and then her forehead.

He pulls her close to him. He says soothing words to comfort her. He knows no matter how hard he tries, she'll always think of her mom and be sad when she does.

"Do you want to go home?"

She shakes her head and wipes her eyes as she pulls back.

I'm OK now. Sorry if I chased her away.

"Who, Bianca?"

She nods.

"Oh babe … you don't need to be sorry. I was happy you needed me. I didn't really want to talk to her for long. The only person I want to talk to is you, and the only person who can call me hottie is you."

Danielle giggles and blushes as she looks at him. He grins as he rests his hand on her cheek and strokes it with the pad of his thumb. She does love him, but one thing bothers her. He said he dated Bianca last year.

Was it during the summer? And only the summer?

Is this thing between us just a summer fling?

She clears her thoughts, as she can't think about that. She knows every relationship is different, and she's going to live this summer day by day and see what happens at the end.

11

THEY'RE BACK

*J*ohn stands on the beach, watching Jacob running around. He took Jacob for a walk for some father-son time before he starts his new job. And even though Danielle and Jacob are supposed to be staying with their grandma without him, he decided to stay with them since his job is only fifteen miles away from her house.

"Daddy, watch me!" Jacob yells as he goes close to the water.

"Jacob, be careful."

As Jacob puts his feet in the water, he doesn't notice the two familiar guys down the beach, walking and kicking sand everywhere while making fun of all the people. They laugh with each other until one of them looks forward and sees Jacob before smirking. He nudges his friend and motions his head toward him. They notice the older guy watching the kid and guess he's the dad, but that doesn't matter to them.

Jacob turns around and stops when he sees them. *Oh no. It's the bad boys of Calm Beach!* He gulps when he sees the smirks but remembers what Trevor said about taking care of it if they bothered them again. *But he's not here!* He turns away from them and runs over to his dad who stares at him, perplexed.

"Whoa, slow down there, champ," John says. "What's the rush?"

"Daddy, we need to go … now!" Jacob tugs on his dad's hand as he watches the guys getting closer to them. "Daddy … please."

"What's wrong, Jacob?" John bends down to look in Jacob's eyes.

Jacob shakes his head. "We have to go, and find Trevor."

"All right., all right," John says as he stands up and takes Jacob's hand. "Lead the way."

He drags his dad away from the beach as fast as he can. The bad boys of Calm Beach, Mark and Ray, stop and laugh as they watch. They love when people are scared of them.

"TREVOR!" Jacob yells after he pushes the door open.

John walks in the house, still puzzled, and closes the door. He turns around to see Danielle walking down the stairs with his mom. They look at him, and he shrugs his shoulders before they all stare at Jacob, concerned.

"Where's Trevor?"

"He's not here today," Grandma Marie says. "He's working."

Jacob's eyes turn to Danielle. "They're back."

She raises her right eyebrow and shrugs, not understanding what he's talking about.

Jacob can see she doesn't get it, so he shakes his head and throws his arms up.

"The bad boys of Calm Beach were at the beach!"

Danielle stares at him in shock. They haven't seen them since the first time they saw them at the start of the summer. She hoped that with Trevor scaring them away, she wouldn't see them again. But she was wrong and needs to warn Trevor.

She reaches into her pocket, taking her phone out and texts him.

> **Danielle:** *Hey. Wanted to warn you that Jacob saw the bad boys of Calm Beach today when he and my dad went to the beach. He's kind of scared.*

Jacob watches Danielle and sees her putting her phone away. He can sense his dad's and grandma's eyes on him. He doesn't want to say anything. Sometimes, he's tired of being a *more mature*—as his teachers said of him—seven-year-old, so he walks away. Danielle follows him leaving John and Grandma Marie watching them. They know Danielle will take care of what's going on, so for now, they let it go.

She finds Jacob sitting on the couch, and she sits down next to him, putting her hand on his shoulder.

He asks, "Did he text you back yet?"

She shakes her head.

The doorbell rings.

Dad will answer it.

But it rings again, so she stands up and walks out of the living room, seeing the entry way abandoned. *Huh. Wonder where they went.*

She shrugs her shoulders and walks over to the door. She opens it to see a very breathless Trevor bending over with his hands on his knees.

"I-is Jacob okay?"

Danielle nods. She steps to the side to let him in. She closes the door. She touches his shoulder and motions at the living room. He nods, and they walk into the living room to see Jacob still sitting on the couch. Jacob looks over at them. His eyes widen as he jumps off the couch and runs over to him, wrapping his arms around his waist.

"Did they do anything to you?" Trevor rests his hand on Jacob's back.

Jacob shakes his head as he looks up. "No, but I think they would have if my daddy wasn't there. They kept staring at me and walking closer, so I ran to Daddy."

"Okay. As long as you're fine," says Trevor as he walks over to the couch and sits down with Jacob's arms still around him. "We have to do something about them."

Danielle sits on the other side of Trevor and rests her hand on his knee, rubbing it with her thumb to calm him down. Trevor puts his hand on hers and gives her a slight smile.

"I know they're called the bad boys of Calm Beach," says Jacob as he lets go of Trevor. "But what did they do to be called that?"

Trevor sighs as he leans back against the couch. "A couple years back, there was a hit-and-run accident. No one knew who did it, but one day, we were arguing, and they spilled that they were the ones in the car. I was in disbelief at first but called the police and told them. They got arrested."

He stops and sees Danielle's and Jacob's shocked faces before he continues, "They only went in for one night and were fined, but it turned out, they were also the ones who had robbed some stores by the beach. They spent about a year in juvie, and now, they're back this summer on probation. No one in Calm Beach can stand them."

Danielle stares at Trevor. She wonders why she's never heard of them since they always come to Calm Beach every summer to visit their grandma. She shrugs as she thinks how it's the same as not meeting Trevor until this summer. She guesses things happen for a reason, but she still wasn't expecting that story.

"But they're afraid of you now because of that?"

Trevor nods his head as he looks at Jacob. "But at the same time, they want to get back at me but won't do it directly. They'll try to get to the people close to me."

He looks over at Danielle. She looks away and looks straight ahead, realizing that they might want to go after her. It was scary the first time she ran into them, and they didn't know she knew Trevor, but now that they do, they might try something bigger next time around.

"Hey. Don't worry." He squeezes her hand. "I won't let them do anything to you. Plus, there's only a month left of the summer. Then, you'll be free from them."

Danielle looks at him and knows he will protect her, no matter the cost. But what he says catches her off guard. There's only one month left, and who knows what will happen between them as they both head to college? She's going to Harvard, and he's heading to Stanford—schools on opposite sides of the country.

I don't know what will happen to us. Will there even be an us when summer ends? I hope so, but something tells me that things won't go as planned. And that scares me.

"Are you okay, Elle?" asks Trevor.

She nods her head and gives him a fake smile. Jacob looks at her and shakes his head, knowing that it's not a genuine smile. And he wants to know why.

"Dani ... that's not a real smile," Jacob says, and Danielle glares at him. "What? It's not, and I want to know why. What's wrong?"

She shakes her head and stands up, walking out of the room. She runs up the stairs to her room and slams the door behind her.

Trevor turns to Jacob after he watches Danielle.

"It was a fake smile?"

Jacob nods his head.

"I'm going to check on her. Will you be okay?"

"I'm seven. Not a baby." Jacob crosses his arms. "Also, Daddy and Grandma are here."

Trevor laughs. "Well … I'm sorry."

He shakes Jacob's hair before he stands up and walks out of the room, following where Danielle went. He jogs up the stairs and over to her bedroom door, knocking on it. Knowing she won't talk out to him, he slowly pushes the door open and sees her lying on the bed. He closes the door and walks over. He bends down to his knees. He leans one arm on the edge of the bed as he reaches his other hand over to stroke Danielle's hair.

"What's wrong?"

Danielle moves her head toward him with tears in her eyes, shaking her head.

"Are you thinking about your mom?"

She shakes her head again.

"Are you worried about Mark and Ray?"

Again, she shakes her head.

Trevor strokes her hair and wipes away a tear. "Are you going to tell me what's wrong?"

Danielle smiles slightly and shakes her head. Trevor smiles, as he can tell that it's a genuine smile. He can see what Jacob saw, and can tell the difference between the one before and the one she's giving him now. He stands up and walks to the edge of the bed before he gets on it. He crawls over to Danielle, lying behind her, and puts his arm around her torso. He pulls her back against him as he moves his lips to her ear.

"Come on," he whispers as he strokes her stomach. "You can tell me."

She sighs and shakes her head. She looks down at the bed, not wanting him to worry about her. And she doesn't want to tell him everything that's on her mind. Not yet.

"All right, you don't have to tell me if you don't want to." He sighs and kisses her cheek before he starts pulling away.

Danielle holds his arm, so he doesn't move. He lies back down, not leaving the spot they're in. He's glad she doesn't want him to. He likes it as he strokes her stomach and kisses the back of her ear before resting his head on the pillow.

He wishes they could stay like this forever, but he knows the summer is going to end. But he also hopes that even though they're going to separate schools, it won't split them up because he loves her and it would hurt him if it did.

She isn't like any of the other girls he's dated.

12

WORK

*W*hile Trevor and Danielle were lying on the bed together a few days ago, he asked her if she would like to see the pizzeria where he worked. She was confused at first because she thought he worked at the hotel, but he explained that his parents wanted him to work elsewhere, so he didn't get bored of the hotel business since he'd be doing that for the rest of his life.

She agreed. He was glad because he wanted to show her how fun it was to make pizza. Also, he wanted to spend as much time with her as possible.

"Ready to go?" asks Trevor.

Danielle was excited when he asked her, but now, she isn't in the mood to go. She has a bad feeling that something is going to go wrong today. She can't shake the feeling. But after some convincing, she agrees. She looks at him and nods.

"You're so lucky, Dani," Jacob says. "I'm just staying home and watching TV."

"I thought kids love watching TV," says Trevor.

"I do." He crosses his arms. "But I'm not in the mood today."

"Well … you can always go to my house and hang out in the game room," Trevor suggests. "We can drop you off on our way."

"No need to do that." Grandma Marie walks in with her purse over her shoulder. "Your mom called and invited Jacob and me to come over. I'll drive us."

"Grandma, you drive?"

"Of course." She looks at Jacob, perplexed. "Why do you ask?"

"I don't know." He shrugs his shoulders. "My friend said his grandma got her keys taken away, so I just thought …"

"I might be a grandma, but I'm only sixty. I choose not to drive all the time," she says. She tries to explain, "Your friend's grandma might have had something happen that worried her family, so they took her keys away for her safety."

"Oh … okay," Jacob says and turns to Trevor and Danielle. "Well then … bye!"

Danielle shakes her head, walks over, and bends down to give him a hug. Then, she goes over to hug Grandma Marie while Trevor shakes Jacob's hair. Jacob pushes Trevor's hand away. Trevor opens the front door. Danielle walks out, and he follows, closing the door behind him.

TREVOR HAS ALREADY MADE a few pizzas while Danielle sits at the counter, watching. He asks her if she wants to help, but each time, she shakes her head. He looks over at her and decides that it is time for her to help. So, he takes some dough and throws it at her when she least expects it. In shock, she looks up at him with wide eyes.

"Oops," he says innocently. "It just slipped."

Danielle stands from the stool and walks around the counter. She reaches her hand toward the counter to grab a hold of some dough and stares back at him with a stern expression that says, *Bring it on*. She throws the dough right at his chest. Trevor looks down at his chest and pushes the dough off him, letting it fall to the floor.

He looks at her as he yells out, "This means war!"

He grabs more dough and starts throwing it at Danielle as she gets flour to retaliate. They continue throwing things at each other while making a mess, but they're laughing and having a good time. After one more throw of flour, Danielle crashes to the floor in laughter. Trevor holds his hand, full of dough, but he drops it to the counter and sits down next to Danielle.

"Now, that was fun." He looks at Danielle, who agrees. "You should come more often."

She giggles as she looks at him.

"Here … you have some dough on your cheek." He leans on one leg as he moves his left hand over to her cheek and slowly wipes it off, bringing it to his lips to lick it. "Tasty."

She smiles as he scoots closer to her, and he strokes her cheek with the pad of his thumb.

"You have more," he whispers as he leans forward to press his lips to her forehead. "Here." He moves his lips down to her cheek. "And here." He glides his lips to her ear as he whispers in her ear, "You taste so damn good."

Danielle shivers as she closes her eyes, loving the sensations of his lips on her. He grins as he lowers his lips down to her jawline. He opens his mouth, letting his tongue glide along, tasting the flour and her silky skin. She moves her head to the side to give him better access as he moves his mouth down to her neck. He leans his body closer to hers. Danielle moans.

Trevor nibbles on her neck before he pulls away, and he looks at her. She opens her eyes and gazes at him with hazy eyes. He loves the way she looks. And knowing that he did that to her makes him love it even more. He rubs his thumb over her lips.

"Now"—he leans back in—"I think I missed a spot. Don't you?"

She looks at him as he rubs her bottom lip and nods her head. He smiles as he rests his other hand on the floor to hold himself steady as he moves his left hand down to hold her chin before closing his eyes. Danielle closes hers. He leans in. And their lips touch. She moves her right hand to his shoulder as their lips move together.

Trevor moves his left hand away from her chin and around to the back of her head to pull her closer to him as their kiss deepens. He grunts as she scoots closer, and she accidentally grazes his manhood with her knee. But that doesn't stop their kiss. He wants to taste her tongue, but as he's about to open his mouth, he hears chuckling.

He unwillingly pulls away from Danielle and looks to his left to see the last two people he wants to see right now—Mark and Ray, aka the bad boys of Calm Beach. They stare down at Trevor and Danielle with smirks along their lips.

"Well, isn't this a cute picture?" Mark says as he continues to smirk. "It's our first victim of the summer and the loser who always tries to ruin everyone's fun."

Trevor pushes himself off the floor. "You two need to leave."

"Or what?" Ray asks as he looks at him up and down. "You gonna call the cops on us again like you did the last time?"

"You two belong in prison." Trevor shakes his head. "Get out."

"Aw, we're just having some fun," says Mark as he glances at Ray. "Right, Ray?"

"Absolutely."

"Come on. Leave, or I'll do something that I'm gonna regret." Trevor wants them to leave the pizzeria and get far away from Danielle.

"Fine. We'll leave. But … we're taking her with us." Mark smirks as he grabs Danielle's arm, pulling her up from the floor and over toward him. "Miss me, babe?"

"Get your filthy hands off her!" Trevor pushes Mark back and pulls Danielle behind him.

Mark steadies himself. "Oh, you really did it this time, Williams."

He stomps over to Trevor and punches him in the face. Trevor wobbles for a moment, but it doesn't take long for him to punch back. Danielle steps back with her eyes wide as she watches them fight. Ray watches them as well and looks at Danielle. He notices her standing there and smirks as he approaches her.

"Hey, baby." He reaches for her hand. "Why don't you come with me? I'll show you a good time. Something that loser over there can never show you."

She snatches her hand away and steps to the right as she tries to get away, but he steps to his left, blocking her. He steps forward. She steps back. He continues to move toward her until she's backed up against the wall. He smirks as he pushes himself up against her.

"Come on, baby." He leans in and whispers in her ear, "It'll be fun. I promise."

Danielle flinches when she feels his lips on her neck. He moves his lips along her skin as he rests his left hand on her waist to hold her still. She squirms as his other hand roams down her body. He smirks against her skin as he finds the bottom of her shirt and creeps his fingers under to touch her skin. Danielle continues trying to fight him off, but he's too strong.

Trevor sees what's happening from the corner of his eye, and he lets all his anger out as he brings his hand back and punches Mark, who falls to the floor. Mark groans as he tries to catch his breath. Trevor turns around and storms over to Danielle. He grabs the back of Ray's shirt and pulls him off her before punching him. He lands on the floor next to Mark.

"Never—and I mean, never—fucking touch her again. Because I swear … you two will never see the light of day," he says as he kicks Ray but stops when he hears sniffling behind him. He turns around. "Elle … are you okay?"

She looks up at him with tears threatening to fall. Trevor's heart breaks, and he reaches out to pull her into his arms. He strokes her back. From that moment on, he swears on his life that he'll never let them or anyone else touch her again.

"I will never let them hurt you again." He pulls away as he puts his hands on either side of her face and strokes her cheeks with his thumbs. "I promise."

Danielle looks him straight in his eyes. She can tell he's telling the truth. She takes a deep breath before leaning up to capture his lips with hers in a much-needed passionate kiss. Trevor moves his hands down to her waist and pulls her as close to him as possible.

When air is needed, they both pull away and stare at each other with love. No words are needed. Trevor smiles and leans back in to press a small kiss on her lips.

"Now … what should we do with them?" He motions his head at Mark and Ray.

Danielle looks over at them and sees them still groaning. *Rightfully so.*

She comes up with a plan. She pulls away from Trevor and walks over to the counter. Trevor watches her, curious. She picks up a large pile of dough and flour before turning around. Then, she walks over to Mark and Ray. She *accidentally* drops the dough onto the guys and sprinkles the flour all over them, leaving them all white.

Trevor watches in amusement. "That's my girl."

Just then, a tall man with a black beard walks in, and his eyes widen at the scene before he exclaims, "What the hell is going on here?"

Trevor turns on his heels when he sees his boss standing on the other side of the counter, looking around. "Mr. Robinson ... I can explain ..."

"Go on."

"Well ... you see," Trevor rubs the back of his neck as he tries to explain, "Danielle and I were having some fun with the pizza-making, and when we got caught up in the moment, Mark and Ray came along —"

"Say no more," Mr. Robinson interrupts him and looks over at Mark and Ray, who are now leaning on their elbows. He turns to Danielle. "Did they hurt you?"

She crosses her arms and looks down as tears form in her eyes again. Trevor sees the tears and walks over to wrap his arms around her to help her feel safe.

"Ray sexually assaulted her," he says to his boss, "against the wall."

"Okay. I'm calling the police," says Mr. Robinson before he walks over to grab the phone and looks at Mark and Ray. "Time for you boys to learn a lesson or two."

They glare up at him and both groan. They're done now. Their probation officers told them that if they messed up one more time, they would end up back in jail and get a longer sentence next time around. They look at each other before Ray looks at Danielle. He's regretting what he did to her. He throws his head back. He's definitely getting a longer sentence time than what Mark will be getting.

THE POLICE COME, take statements from Trevor and Danielle, and take Mark and Ray away in their cars, off to the jail. One stays behind to tell Trevor and Danielle that they might have to testify if it goes to trial. He nods his head but he isn't sure how Danielle will be able to since she isn't speaking. But maybe she'll talk by then.

Danielle looks at Trevor and sighs, knowing what he's thinking. She looks down understanding they will need her to speak to do so but she's not ready.

"Hey." He places his fingers under her chin, lifting her head up so he's gazing in her eyes. "Whether you're speaking or not, I won't make you talk about what happened. You shouldn't have to relive what that pig put you through."

She smiles slightly at him. She can tell he cares for her more than he's cared for anyone else in his life. How? Because she senses it. And it makes her feel special.

"I care about you, Elle," he says as he strokes her chin, "more than you know."

She wraps her arms around his neck. He rests his hands on her waist as they try forgetting the awful stuff that happened that day. The one officer who is still in the pizzeria smiles at the young couple before looking away. Trevor leans down to capture Danielle's lips with his. She smiles against his lips as she moves her hand to the back of his head, pulling him closer. She runs her fingers through his hair as their bodies touch.

When she needs air, Danielle pulls back. Trevor rests his forehead against hers.

"This has been the best summer of my life so far," says Trevor.

She nods in agreement. He leans in and gives her another peck on her lips. They pull away from each other, and Trevor laces their hands together. After everything that happened, Mr. Robinson lets Trevor go home for the day. So, they walk out of the pizzeria and decide to leave this day behind them for now as they head to Danielle's house.

13

ORIENTATION LETTERS

"*M*ail's here!" Jacob yells from the bottom of the stairs.

He can hear footsteps, and he looks up to see his sister running down the stairs toward him. She stops and grabs the mail from Jacob, flipping through them until she finds the right one. She gives Jacob back the rest of the mail. She turns the envelope over and rips the seal as Grandma Marie and John walk over.

They watch her with proud smiles, knowing her Harvard's orientation letter has come. It's been her dream to go there, and she will now know when. John and their mom were never the parents to force their kids to do something they didn't want to do. Danielle's eyes skim over the words she's been waiting to read and grins.

John walks over and looks over her shoulder as he says, "*Congratulations! We are pleased to officially welcome you to Harvard University. Your New Student Orientation will be held September 1 through 3, 2021.*"

Grandma Marie grins as she walks over to hug Danielle. "Congratulations again, sweetie. I know how hard you worked, and your mom would be so proud of you. As we are."

Danielle nods as she pulls away and stares back down at the paper, but then she feels two small arms around her torso.

"Are you going to leave me?"

She sees Jacob looking up at her with a worried expression.

She gives him a slight smile as she kneels down to his size, wrapping her arms around him to give him a big hug. She looks at her dad for help to explain as she pulls away.

"Jacob, we talked about this a few months ago. Dani will be going to study at a bigger school, called Harvard University. It is one of the top schools in the country," says John as he looks at Jacob. "She isn't leaving you. Harvard is only five hours away by car. We can always take trips to see her, and she'll come home every holiday."

Jacob looks at Danielle, hopeful, as he asks, "You will?"

She nods and gets another hug from him, but this time, it is much tighter. She almost loses her balance. She can understand why he's holding on to her, but as much as she loves her little brother, she wants him to let go.

"All right, sweetie." Grandma Marie walks over and touches Jacob's shoulder. "I think it's time to let her go. She has some news to text someone. Why don't you come with me, and we will make cookies to celebrate?"

"Okay," he says as he lets go of Danielle and walks toward the kitchen.

"Go ahead, sweetie." John motions his head at the stairs. "Go text your boy."

Danielle rolls her eyes to let him know he isn't funny. John shrugs his shoulders as he laughs. She turns, takes two steps at a time and walks into her room. She jumps on her bed and reaches for her cell phone. Then, she types as she lies on her stomach.

Danielle: *Hey. I got my orientation letter!*

She presses Send and puts her phone down on her bed. She rolls over to lie on her back and rests the letter on her stomach. She stares up at the ceiling and puts her thumb up, hoping her mom sees. She closes her eyes.

DANIELLE FLUTTERS HER EYES OPEN. She brings her hand to her eyes, rubbing them to get them adjusted to the light. She pushes herself up onto her elbows and looks down to the end of her bed, where she sees Trevor sitting. *When did he get here?*

She can tell he's thinking hard about something and follows where his eyes are looking to see an envelope in his hands. *Stanford.* She bites her lip as she closes her eyes, not ready to find out when he's leaving.

She reopens her eyes and takes a silent breath before she pushes herself down her bed and sits right next to him. Trevor can sense her sitting next to him, but he doesn't look at her.

"I got my orientation letter, too, but I wanted to open it with you." He sighs and turns to her. "But you were sleeping, and I didn't want to wake you."

Danielle puts her hand on his shoulder as she mouths, *It'll be okay.*

"I hope you're right," he says. "I wanted to officially congratulate you on getting into Harvard. I know how much you want to go there, and you deserve it. It's your dream, and I want you to have all the dreams in the world."

She smiles but still feels sad, deep down knowing that even though she's going to live her dream, Trevor might not be in it. Her dreams have changed since finding out he's going to school thousands of miles away. She wants to be with him, but she knows he won't let her give up her dream. She looks down.

Trevor knows what she's thinking about. He can read her better than anyone. He turns to her and moves his fingers under her chin to lift her head. He leans in, capturing Danielle's lips with his. He needs to distract her. He wants her to stop thinking. And … she does. She moves her hand to the back of his head, letting her fingers run through his hair to deepen the kiss.

He nibbles her lower lip before pulling away. "I knew that would work."

He pecks her lips. She opens her eyes and giggles, shaking her head. She puts her arm through his and rests her head on his shoulder. She looks down at the envelope sitting in his lap. He laces their fingers and gives her hand a slight squeeze.

"I guess it's time to find out, huh?"

He takes a deep breath and looks at the envelope. He unlaces their fingers, so he can use both hands to open it. Danielle watches with curious eyes as she takes a deep breath. Trevor opens and pulls the letter out.

He reads it out loud,

"Dear Trevor Williams …" He glances at Danielle before continuing, *"We are pleased to officially welcome you to Stanford. Your New Student Orientation will be held August 25 through 27, 2021 …"*

He stops talking and tosses the letter and envelope to the floor. Danielle looks up at him with tears in her eyes. He turns to her and uses the pad of his thumbs to wipe the tears away. He leans forward and kisses her cheek. He reaches for her phone, handing it to her because he wants to hear what she thinks.

"Write what you feel."

She takes it and starts typing.

> Congratulations. You deserve it!

Trevor sighs. "No. I want to know how you really feel."

> I'm happy for you, Trev. I'm sure your parents will be proud to know it's official and coming so soon.

"But what do you want?"

> It's not about what I want. Do I like that it's happening so soon? No, but it's not about me. You want to make your parents proud, and going to Stanford will do that.

He looks down, knowing she's right, and looks back at her. "But what if I've changed my mind? What if I want to withdraw and go to Harvard with you? I got in there too."

Danielle sighs.

> But is that what you want? I don't want to be the reason for you to change your mind. Just as I know you wouldn't want to be the reason if I ever changed my mind. I care about you. I know you love your parents. You should go to Stanford.

Trevor nods in agreement. She's right. He wouldn't want her to give up her dream for him, but it's different. Isn't it?

Just wish it wasn't coming so fast.

He shrugs his shoulders as he looks at Danielle and then leans in, giving her a much-needed passionate kiss. She smiles against his lips as she puts her hands on his neck, and he shifts her, so he can rest his hand on her waist.

Even though they don't know what will happen with their relationship when they go off to different colleges, they still have one month left of summer, and they won't let this bump or worry ruin the last moments they have with each other.

1 4

HEART ATTACK

*J*acob and Danielle lie next to each other on the grass while their dad is at work and Grandma Marie is inside. Trevor is at work, and Danielle isn't ready to go back to the pizzeria yet after what happened with Mark and Ray. So, she decided to spend the day with Jacob since they haven't spent too much one-on-one time lately, and after summer is over, she's not so sure how much time she'll be seeing him because of school. She doesn't want Jacob to feel like she's leaving him.

"I'm going to see what Grandma is doing," Jacob says randomly. Then, he jumps up from the grass and walks into the house, looking around. "Grandma?"

He doesn't see her in the kitchen so he walks around the house, confused because he can't find her. But as he reaches the bottom of the stairs, he hears groaning, so he jogs up the stairs to follow the sound. The groaning gets louder, and Jacob wonders if he should get Danielle, but he continues to follow the sound and ends up standing in front of Grandma Marie's door. He pushes it open and sees her lying on her bed, breathing heavily.

"Grandma?" He runs over to the side of the bed. "Grandma, what's wrong with you?!"

Grandma Marie turns her head and whispers, "Sweetie, go get your sister."

"Dani!" screams Jacob as he runs out of the room, down the stairs, and out to the back.

He runs over to Danielle, and she looks up at him, puzzled, when he grabs her hand, pulling her up from the ground. He runs into the house, dragging Danielle along with him. They run up the stairs and into Grandma Marie's room. Danielle stops as she stares at her grandma on the bed, breathing heavily and holding her chest. She's worried because she's never seen her like this. She runs over to the bed.

"Sweetie," Grandma Marie whispers, "I think I'm having a heart attack. Can you get the ambulance here?"

Danielle widens her eyes. Her grandma is having a heart attack. She looks around the room as she tries to figure out how to get an ambulance to them … fast. Tears fill up her eyes as she thinks about all the different outcomes. She can't lose another person. Not now.

One idea comes to mind, and she takes out her cell phone and texts Trevor.

Danielle: *I need you. Grandma is having a heart attack. I can't call an ambulance, and Jacob … is just staring at her. Please. I can't lose someone else.*

She gazes down at her grandma and reaches out to take her hand. Danielle squeezes it to let her know that she's not alone. A few moments later, she can sense the vibration of her phone, so she uses her other hand to look at it.

Trevor: *The ambulance is on its way. I'm coming too. Stay put.*

Danielle reads it as tears fall down her cheeks. She puts her phone away and looks at Grandma Marie. She can't believe this or deal with it. Not now. She lost her mom a couple months ago. And now, her grandma is having a heart attack.

Please, God, don't take my grandma away.

Trevor ... please get here as fast as you can.

DANIELLE HATES WAITING ROOMS. She sat in a bunch of them during the last few months of her mom's life as they waited for the day to come to say good-bye. And now, she's in one again with the company of Jacob, Trevor, her dad, and Trevor's parents, who were called on the way to the hospital.

She rests her head on Trevor's shoulder as she cries. He has his arm around her torso while his other arm is around Jacob, who is sobbing into Trevor's chest. Trevor has tears in his own eyes. Grandma Marie became like another grandma to him, and just as much as everyone else, he doesn't want to lose her.

"I'm going to get coffee." John stands up. "Anyone want anything?"

"John, sit down." Joe stands, shaking his head. He looks at him. "I'll get some coffee. You sit and relax."

"I'm fine," he says in a soft tone.

Danielle watches her dad, concerned. He's acting similar to how he acted when her mom was dying. He always wanted to act strong around her and Jacob, and she knows that. She wishes though that he would take time for himself instead of always worrying about them.

"Then, we'll come with you." Sarah rises from her chair and looks at Trevor. "Will you three be okay for a couple of minutes?"

"Yeah, Mom, we'll be fine," says Trevor as he pulls Danielle and Jacob closer to him.

John, Joe, and Sarah walk out of the waiting room to find some coffee. Jacob rubs his face a little on Trevor before looking up at Danielle.

"Is Grandma going to be okay?"

She gives him a weak smile as she grabs his hand over Trevor's stomach and starts rubbing her thumb on the back of his hand. This is what she always did when they sat together, waiting on news about their mom, but this time, she isn't alone. She has Trevor there to keep her calm and be strong for her little brother.

"You two should go to sleep," says Trevor. "I'll wake you if anything happens."

They agree. Jacob shifts and lays his head on Trevor's lap, and then he closes his eyes. Danielle lays her head on Trevor's chest while placing her hand on Jacob's back and stares at a wall. Trevor knows she's still awake, so he rubs her back up and down and kisses the top of her head. She slowly closes her eyes.

A woman gently shakes Danielle's arm. "Danielle ... Ellie-Bear."

Danielle flutters her eyes open and widens them when she sees her. "Mom?!"

She looks around, puzzled, as she's still in the waiting room with Trevor's arm wrapped around her. But no one is moving. No one but her and her mom.

"How is this possible?" asks Danielle as she slowly moves Trevor's arm from around her and stands up, staring at her. "Mom ... you died."

"Sweetie, this is just a dream," she says as she walks over to place her hands on Danielle's shoulders. "Ellie, I'm so proud of you. And of your brother. For being able to cope and move on from my death."

"Mommy ... I won't talk to anyone but you." Danielle looks down. "How is that being able to cope? Or how does that show I've moved on? I haven't ..."

Her mom rests her fingers under Danielle's chin and lifts her head, so they look eye to eye with each other. "Honey, that doesn't matter. All that matters is that you're happy, and I can see that boy Trevor is one reason you are. And I couldn't be more thrilled to know that my baby girl is happy even if she doesn't believe it."

"Do I love him?"

Her mom smiles. "That is up to you to decide, sweetie ... Danielle, wake up."

"Mom?" asks Danielle as her mom starts to fade away. "Mom?!"

"Honey, wake up."

DANIELLE GROANS as someone is shaking her, and she fights to stay asleep. *No. Sleep. Mom.*

But the person doesn't stop, so she grunts as she opens her eyes and looks up. She sees her dad looking down at her with a grin.

"Grandma is in her room. Awake and alert. She wants to see you."

She rubs her eyes before she slowly pushes herself off Trevor, who she finds sleeping with his head back against the wall. She lowers her hand down to ease his arm from her waist, and she stands up. She straightens her pants before hugging her dad. He rubs her back and says soothing words in her ear, something she needs. They pull back, and he gives her directions on how to get to the room. She nods and walks down the hall.

Danielle follows the directions her dad told her and stands in front of a door. She puts her hand on the knob and leans forward to rest her forehead against it, hesitating. The last time she opened a hospital door was the last time she saw her mom alive.

But it's different this time around. Right?

She won't know until she opens the door. She backs away and pushes the door open looking straight at the bed to see her grandma's eyes open.

"Hi, sweetie," says Grandma Marie. "Come on over."

Danielle walks over and leans in to give her a hug before sitting down in a chair next to the bed. She scoots it closer to the bed. Grandma Marie looks at her and reaches over to take her hand.

"I'm okay," she says. "You saw your mom, didn't you?"

Danielle stares at her in shock. *She knows?* She bites her lower lip in confusion. *How could she possibly know about the dream? The dream that felt so real.*

She nods her head, and tears form in her eyes again. She's sick of crying.

"I know. I saw her too," Grandma Marie explains. "While I was in surgery, she came to visit me in my dreams. She helped me survive the heart attack. Dani, honey, she was really there. She told me she would visit you next. She wants you to be happy."

Danielle nods her head as she wipes the tears away, knowing she's right.

"And Trevor makes you happy. We all see it, and I know you see it too," says Grandma Marie as she strokes the back of Danielle's hand. "I know you're scared, but I also know you love him; you need to decide if you love him enough to make it work after summer."

Danielle now starts sobbing for more than one reason: one, she can't understand how her grandma is focusing on her instead of herself, and two, she doesn't know what to do. She knows she and her mom are right, but does she want to have a long-distance relationship with a guy she had a thing with over the summer?

She shakes her head. It's more than a "thing," and she only has a few weeks left before she has to make one of the toughest decisions of her life. She loves him. She knows it. But she doesn't want to say it in case he leaves for school and they never see each other again.

15

OLD FRIEND

*A*fter a three-day hospital stay, Grandma Marie is now home, resting in her own comfortable bed, recovering from her heart attack. She told everyone that she didn't want them to worry about her that day, as she'd spend most of it sleeping, so she made John go back to work and sent Danielle and Jacob off to spend the day with Trevor.

"What do you want to do today, buddy?" asks Trevor as he holds Danielle's hand.

Jacob shrugs his shoulders. "I don't know."

Danielle looks around as they walk along the beach. She senses she's being watched, but it's not creepy. It's more like it's familiar. She continues to look around as Trevor and Jacob talk to each other. She stops when she sees a familiar face and is in shock.

Trevor notices her stopping, so he looks at her. "Elle, you okay?"

"Daniclle?!" A dark-skinned girl around the same age of Danielle and Trevor look over at them and lets out a squeal as she runs over and hugs Danielle tightly. "Oh my God, it is you! I thought I'd never see you again."

Danielle giggles as she pulls away. Jacob stares at the person with his head to the side because he feels like he has seen her before. But where?

The girls look at him.

"Don't tell me that's the same kid we used to watch all the time?"

Danielle nods. The girl bends down and picks Jacob up, giving him a tight hug, leaving him even more confused. He looks over at Danielle with his mouth open, and she gives him a thumbs-up, letting him know it's okay. He is put back down on the ground, and the girl turns to Danielle, puzzled.

"Why aren't you saying anything?" She puts one hand on her waist as she raises her right eyebrow. "I mean ... we used to never stop talking. So, what gives?"

Danielle sighs as she pulls out her phone.

Long story short, my mom passed away a couple weeks before summer. The last words I said to her were ,"I love you," and I haven't said anything since.

"Oh my God ... I'm so sorry! I loved your mom, and I know how close the two of you were ... well, how close the whole family is," she says as she wraps her arms around Danielle. She sees Trevor next to Jacob and whispers, "Damn. Who's that hottie?"

Danielle pulls back from the hug and smiles. She backs up and reaches for Trevor's hand, pulling him close to her. He lets her hand go and wraps his arm around her waist, letting it rest right above her hip as he pulls her to his side.

"Is he your boyfriend?" The girl wiggles her eyebrows.

Danielle nods as she types.

Yes. Britney, this is my boyfriend, Trevor. Trevor, this is one of my old friends from middle and high school, Britney.

They both read it. Jacob jumps up, so he can get a better look, and Danielle lowers it, so he can read it. His mouth opens wide as some memories come back to him. He sighs in relief, knowing he wasn't hugging a random person.

Trevor puts his right hand out. "It's nice to meet you."

"You too," says Britney as she shakes his hand. She looks at Danielle, giving her a nod of approval. "Very nice choice."

Danielle rolls her eyes. Britney used to bug Danielle about not having a boyfriend, but it never bothered her that she didn't have one. Danielle and Britney were good friends throughout middle school and high school until Britney had to move during junior year. They didn't keep in touch unless it was comments here and there on Facebook or Instagram.

"So, what are you beautiful people doing?"

Jacob shrugs his shoulders. "We don't know what to do."

"Well, you can always hang here on the beach." She sees their faces drop at her suggestion. "Ah, you're here all the time?"

Danielle nods.

"Same old family." Britney giggles and then says, "I don't really know what else there is to do around here other than the beach."

"Let's hang out here," says Trevor as he grins at Danielle. "It'll be fun."

She shrugs her shoulders and mouths, *Okay.*

Trevor kisses her cheek and looks at Britney. "Would you like to join us?"

"Sure ... I've got nothing better to do, and I totally need to catch up with Danielle."

"All right! Let's find a good spot to lie around," he says as he leaves his arm around Danielle's waist, and they all walk side by side on the beach.

TREVOR KICKS the sand and water over at Jacob, who laughs before doing it back, while Danielle and Britney sit on beach chairs, talking about memories and catching up.

"So, how did you meet Trevor?"

Danielle smiles as she types.

The second day of summer, Jacob and I were at the beach, and Trevor accidentally bumped into me. He apologized, but then I thought I made myself look like a fool in front of him because of the not-talking thing, so I ran away. He ended up bringing Jacob home and came up to my room to talk. And there it is. OH! Then, the next day, he saved Jacob and me from the bad boys of Calm Beach, who harassed us.

"Aw, I love *bumping into each other* stories. It's a great way to meet, except the part about the bad boys, but ya know what I mean." Britney giggles but then questions, "Do you think you'll ever talk again?"

IDK. I want the first words I say to be *"I love you,"* but I'm not ready to say them.

"You mean, to Trevor?"

Danielle nods, resting her head back against the chair, and puts her phone next to her. Britney smiles at her before putting her head back. They stare at the water to see the boys coming over to them. Trevor's eyes connect with Danielle's, and he grins as he sits down on the edge of her chair. He takes her hand and kisses the tips of her fingers. She blushes and then scoots over to make room, and he pushes himself back to sit with her. He puts his arm around her, and she snuggles close to him, resting her right hand on his stomach.

"Hey." Jacob looks at them and pouts. "What about me?"

Trevor laughs and pulls Danielle closer to him. She slaps his chest before pulling herself away as she shifts to leave some space between them. She looks at Jacob and taps the empty space. He grins as he jumps onto the chair and gets comfortable.

"Look at the beautiful family," says Britney and takes out her phone. "Picture time!"

Danielle rolls her eyes at Britney. Britney laughs as she moves her legs over the edge of the chair and stands up. She walks to the far end of Danielle's chair, holding her phone up. Trevor, Jacob, and Danielle look at her and give her their best smiles.

"Perfect," says Britney. She types on her phone and looks at Danielle. "Just sent it you."

Danielle smiles and mouths, *Thank you.*

Britney looks at her phone. "Oh, I should go. I have to do something for my mom."

She walks over to the chair. She bends down to give Trevor and Jacob a hug and then leans over to give Danielle a hug. "We definitely need to hang out before summer ends."

Danielle nods in agreement as Britney pulls away. They say their good-byes before she puts her phone to her ear and walks away. Danielle smiles, watching her, and looks at Trevor to see him staring back at her.

"She's nice," he says, "but of course, not as nice as my amazing girlfriend."

She giggles and blushes. He grins. He loves making her blush, and he loves when she giggles. One day, he knows he'll love her voice too. He pushes Jacob's head down as he leans over to take Danielle's lips to his. Jacob turns away, disgusted. Trevor raises his hand to stroke Danielle's cheek as their lips move together.

Jacob groans as he covers his eyes. "Ew. Stop! That's gross."

Trevor pulls away, and he looks down at Jacob. "Sorry, little man. I guess we got carried away. But blame your sister for being irresistible."

Danielle gasps but blushes as she playfully slaps Trevor's chest.

"What?" He leans forward and whispers huskily, "It's true. I can't get enough of you."

"Gross. Gross. Gross!" says Jacob as he jumps off the chair and onto the chair that Britney was sitting in. "I'm glad I don't have a girlfriend. Girls are gross."

"You'll change your mind when you're older," says Trevor as he gazes at Danielle and strokes her cheek and then her lips with the pad of his thumb, "especially when you meet the girl of your dreams, like I did."

And again, she blushes. She knows that the next few weeks will be the best weeks of her life, as she's already declared the summer being as one of the best she's had in a long time, even with the few bumps along the way.

BRIAN AND CRAIG

*T*revor leans his elbows on the counter in the pizzeria as he waits for customers to come in. It's been a slow day, and ever since the day Mark and Ray got arrested, his boss has been taking it easy on him by having someone else make the pizzas while Trevor runs the counter. He is bored. But he sees the door open, and in walks two guys he didn't think he'd see this summer. He stands up straight with a smile.

"Well, well, well, look who it is," says the guy with spiky black hair and a smirk as they walk over to the counter. "It's the loser who's been ditching us this summer."

"Not ditching." Trevor chuckles as he shakes his head. "Just busy."

"Right. Just busy," the tall, dark-skinned male says sarcastically. "I don't believe that for one second. Do you, Brian?"

"Not at all, Craig."

"All right. Shut up, assholes." Trevor rolls his eyes. "Did you two come for food or to annoy me?"

"Nah, we're here for food," says Brian, "but also wanted to see if you were here. We're wondering what you've been up to since we haven't seen you around, like, at all."

"Yeah, well, like I said, I've been busy," he says with a shrug. "What do you guys want?"

"We'll take two pies. One with pepperoni and one with mushrooms," says Craig, and he looks back at Brian, who nods in agreement, "and we'll have two colas with that."

"For here or to go?"

"For here."

"You're going to eat a pie each?"

"You've seen how much we can eat when we're hungry." Brian laughs. "No, we won't eat it all. I'll probably bring the rest to my parents or something."

"Got it," says Trevor as he puts the order in the register and writes it down on a piece of paper. Then, he turns around to place it in the open window. "New order!"

Craig raises his right eyebrow as he asks, "Not making pizzas today?"

"Nope. My boss has been taking it easy on me this past week," explains Trevor as he shrugs his shoulders, "ever since the thing with Mark and Ray."

"Whoa, back up. What thing?" asks Brian.

"You haven't heard?"

Brian and Craig shake their heads in confusion.

"Where have you two been? Under a rock?"

"I guess … not paying attention?" Brian shrugs his shoulders. "So, what happened?"

"Hold on." Trevor turns around and calls out to his coworker, "Hey, Ben, when the next order comes out, I'm going on my break. That okay?"

Ben nods in agreement. "Sure, man. I got this."

"Thanks, man." He turns around. "I'll join you guys when your order comes out."

"All right," says Craig.

Trevor smiles. He's not sure how much he should tell them. Yes, the three of them have known each other since forever, but could he tell them about Danielle? Why wouldn't he? Because he's not sure how they would react to her not talking or the fact that he has a girlfriend when all he used to talk about was enjoying the last summer before college without dating.

So, the question is, *do I tell them everything or leave Danielle out of it?*

Brian notices that Trevor is in deep thought. "Hey, man. You all right?"

He shakes his head, clearing his thoughts. "Oh, yeah … just thinking."

DANIELLE POINTS the remote at the TV pressing the channel button, bored but calm at the same time. When she settles on a channel, she throws the remote on the couch and leans back against the cushions. Grandma Marie enters the living room and sits on the couch, opening the newspaper to read, while Jacob sits on the floor with his legs crossed, a crayon in hand to color a picture of a dog.

Jacob looks up at Danielle. "Where's Trevor?"

She looks at him but then at Grandma Marie to answer for her, who nods as she puts down her paper and says, "He's probably at work."

"Oh," says Jacob before he goes back to coloring. But then he asks, "Where does he work?"

"He works at a pizza place. Why?"

"Just asking." He shrugs his shoulders. "I'm hungry. Can we go visit him and get pizza?"

Grandma Marie looks at Danielle, who shakes her head, sighing, as she's not ready to go back. All she can think about is how uncomfortable she was when being held up against the wall. Trevor, Grandma Marie, and her dad all understand that, but she isn't sure Jacob does.

"Honey," says Grandma Marie as she looks at Jacob, "why don't we order it?"

"But, Grandma," Jacob whines, "I want to go see where Trevor works!"

"Jacob, do you remember when your dad and I explained to you about what happened with the bad boys of Calm Beach, as you call them, and Trevor and Danielle?"

Jacob nods.

"Well, that happened at the pizza place, and she's not ready to go back there yet."

"Ohhh," says Jacob before he looks at Danielle. "Sorry."

She gives him a slight smile and reaches for her phone.

If Jacob wants to go, you two can go. Bring me back a couple slices?

Grandma Marie reads it. "Are you sure?"

Danielle nods.

Grandma Marie smiles as she looks at Jacob. "Jacob, do you want to get that pizza?"

"But I thought ..."

"Danielle said we can go, and we'll bring her back some."

"Are you sure?" He glances at Danielle, and she nods in agreement, so he drops his crayon before jumping up. He turns to Grandma Marie. "All right ... let's go!"

"Dude, I can't believe they did that. I mean, I know they're idiots, but that's low," says Brian as he shakes his head and takes a sip from his soda. "Man, if I saw them on the street, I'd beat the crap out of them myself."

"Same here." Craig nods in agreement. "How's the girl? Danielle's her name?"

"Yeah," says Trevor. "She's okay. I mean … she's shaken up."

"I'm sure," says Brian. "Who wouldn't be?"

Craig looks at Trevor and asks, "Have you seen her again?"

Before Trevor can open his mouth, he hears a familiar boy's voice yelling out, "Trevor!"

He turns and rests his hand on the top of his chair as he sees Grandma Marie and Jacob walking into the pizzeria. He grins as he stands up and walks over to them. He hugs Grandma Marie and high-fives Jacob. Brian and Craig watch and then look at each other, curious.

"What are you doing here?"

"I was hungry," says Jacob, "and I wanted to see you too!"

"Well, I'm honored." Trevor laughs. "Where's your sister?"

Grandma Marie sighs. "She's still not ready to come back here yet but told us we could come and to make sure we bring her back food."

"I understand," he says. "Well, I'm on a break, but Ben is taking orders. Oh, and my boss said that anything your family orders from now on is on the house."

"He doesn't have to do that."

"I know, but that's the kind of guy he is."

"All right, I'm going to go get our food." Grandma Marie looks at Jacob. "Are you going to come to the counter with me?"

"No," he answers. "I want to wait with Trevor."

Grandma Marie shakes her head and looks at Trevor, who laughs as he nods.

"It's okay. He can wait with me if he wants."

"You're too good to him sometimes."

Jacob looks up at her with his eyes wide, and Trevor chuckles as he puts his right hand on Jacob's shoulder. "Come on, little man. Let's go sit down while your grandma orders the food. I know how your sister gets when she's hungry."

"True that!"

Trevor laughs and pushes Jacob forward. "Come on."

He turns around and sees his two friends staring at him. *Right. Forgot about them.*

With Jacob here with him, Trevor will have to tell them about Danielle now. And again, he's not sure how they will take it since that's the main reason he hasn't been around all summer.

Trevor glances down to Jacob and back at the table before taking a slight breath. He walks over to the table. He sits back down on the wooden chair as Jacob sits down next to him. Brian and Craig move their eyes from Jacob to Trevor and then back to Jacob.

"Hello," says Brian.

"Hi!" says Jacob with enthusiasm. "Who are you?"

"He's Brian," says Craig as he motions his head at Brian, "and I'm Craig."

"Cool. I'm Jacob," he says. "I'm Trevor's little buddy."

Brian raises his eyebrow as he glances at Trevor. "Is that so?"

"Yep!" Jacob nods his head and looks at Trevor. "Right?"

"Right, little man."

Jacob grins as he looks back at Brian and Craig. "I'm also Danielle's little brother!"

"Danielle?" Craig now raises his own eyebrow as he looks at Trevor, both confused and curious. "You mean, the girl who—"

Before he can continue his question, Trevor interrupts him and nods, "Yes. I guess I forgot to mention that I knew Danielle before that day. She's ... she's my girlfriend."

"Girlfriend?" Brian looks at him, surprised. "You have a girlfriend? This summer?"

"Yes."

"Wow." Craig sits back in his chair in shock. "I mean, that's awesome. Now, we get why you've been busy this summer. Now that I think about it, Bianca mentioned something about you seeing someone but wasn't sure how long it would last after she saw you."

"Yeah, well, we all know how Bianca thinks about a lot of things," says Brian as he rolls his eyes, "especially when it comes to ex-boyfriends."

Jacob looks at the three guys, feeling out of place. He doesn't know what they are talking about and doesn't think he wants to know. This isn't what he had in mind when he wanted to visit Trevor at the pizza place. *How was I supposed to know Trevor would have friends here?*

He rests his hands together on the table, and he rocks back and forth, bored.

Craig looks at him, chuckling. "You okay?"

"Yeah." Jacob shrugs his shoulders.

Trevor turns to Jacob and can tell he's not okay. Not only has he learned how to read Danielle better, but he's also learned how to read Jacob. "Jacob, what's up?"

"I don't know." He shrugs again and looks at Trevor. "I'm hungry and bored."

"That's all?"

"Yes." Jacob nods and looks at Brian and Craig. "You two look funny."

"Funny?" Brian moves his head to the side. "Funny how?"

"I don't know. You have funny faces."

Trevor chuckles as he sees his two friends stare at Jacob with their mouths open. He knows that sometimes, Jacob cracks a joke if he doesn't want to talk about something. Trevor thinks he has an idea what's wrong. Hanging out with his friends isn't what Jacob had in mind when he came to the pizzeria. Trevor didn't even expect his day to go like this, getting visitors. But he's glad he did.

He looks back at Brian and Craig, and starts laughing as he sees the two making funny faces at Jacob. "What are you two doing?"

"Your little buddy here said we had funny faces, so we decided to make them funnier," Brian explains as he shrugs his shoulders.

"Interesting," says Trevor before looking at Jacob. "How's your sister today?"

"She's good. She was watching something when we left. I think she was bored."

"Gotcha," says Trevor. "Maybe I'll come by after work, and we can do something."

Jacob's eyes lighten up as he asks, "All three of us?"

"Yep. All three of us."

Brian and Craig glance at each other, knowing they're thinking the same thing. They knew their friend was good with kids, but they didn't realize he was this good. They look up and notice the gray-haired woman, who Jacob came with, is walking toward their table.

"All right, Jacob." Grandma Marie looks at them. "It's time to go home."

"Already, Grandma?"

"Yes. I should go rest a little," she answers, "and I'm sure Danielle is hungry."

"Fine." Jacob reluctantly gets off the chair and turns to Trevor. "See you later, right?"

"Right." He gives him a high five and looks at Grandma Marie. "I hope you don't mind, but I told him I'd come over after work, and we would do something together with Elle."

"You know you don't have to ask to come over." She shakes her head and smiles at all three of them. "Well, I hope you three enjoy your day, and we'll see you later, Trevor."

"Yes, Marie, and thank you."

Brian and Craig give her a smile as they, too, say, "Thank you," and "Good-bye."

Grandma Marie and Jacob walk out of the pizzeria, with Jacob holding the door open. Trevor watches them before turning around to see Brian and Craig staring at him.

"What?"

"Girlfriend?" Brian raises his eyebrow as he gives him a *really* look. "I thought you weren't getting involved with anyone this summer since it's the last one before college."

Trevor shrugs his shoulders. "I wasn't looking for one, but things happen."

"How'd you meet her?" asks Craig.

Jacob pushes the door open, walking into the house, and waits for Grandma Marie to come in before closing the door. They move farther into the house and into the living room to see Danielle still sitting on the couch, watching TV. She glances over to see they're back, so she picks up the remote to turn it off. She stands up and walks over to them.

"Hungry?" Grandma Marie holds up the pizza box in her hand. "I bought a pie—half-plain and half-pepperoni."

Danielle smiles and nods. They go through the house and into the kitchen. Danielle walks over and opens the cabinets to take out three plates. After closing the cabinet door, she puts the plates on the table as Jacob grabs the napkins, placing them on the table before he sits down on one of the dining room chairs. Grandma Marie puts the pizza box in the middle of the table and takes a seat. Danielle sits down on the chair across from Jacob. They each grab a slice.

Jacob looks at Danielle. "Trevor said he would come over when he's done working."

She nods with a smile before taking a bite of her pepperoni slice.

"He also had a couple friends there," he continues talking, "Brian and Craig. They're funny-looking, especially when they make funny faces."

Danielle raises her eyebrow at Grandma Marie, feeling perplexed. Trevor has never mentioned a Brian or a Craig before; he's never mentioned any of his friends, except when they ran into his ex-girlfriend. She is wondering why.

"They seem like nice boys," says Grandma Marie. "They also seem like they've known each other for a while. Has Trevor ever mentioned them?"

Danielle shakes her head as she takes another bite. *I wonder why he's never mentioned his friends or why he has said nothing about hanging out with them or wanting to. I hope he doesn't feel like he can't hang out with them to be with me ...*

"Honey"—Grandma Marie stares at Danielle, who looks deep in thought—"are you okay?"

Danielle gives her a smile as she nods before taking another bite.

TREVOR WATCHES his two friends continue eating their pizza. He stole a slice before and finished telling them about Danielle and how they'd met. He left out the part about her not talking. He doesn't want them thinking she's weird or anything. Because she's not.

"So, do you think you and Danielle will make it after summer, or is this just a summer fling?" asks Brian to break the silence.

Trevor sighs. "I don't know. I want to, and I think she does, too, but she's going to Harvard, and I'm going to Stanford. It would be hard."

"True," says Craig, "but it's been done before."

"Our situation is a little different from others."

Brian looks at him with his head to the side. "What do you mean?"

"I forgot to tell you … she doesn't speak," he says, and they stare at him with confused eyes. "She's been through some stuff, and she stopped talking afterward."

Brian asks, "How do you communicate?"

"She uses the Notes app on her phone, and we text a lot when we're not together."

"Wow," says Craig. "Now, I get why it could be difficult to do long-distance."

"I still think you could do it," Brian claims. "I mean, if you really like her. You shouldn't let the country between you two stop you.

Also, you can change your mind about Stanford. We know it's not your first choice, and you're only going 'cause of your parents."

"I know. But I'm happy they're letting me go to college instead of going right into the business even if it is Stanford," says Trevor before sighing. "But I don't want to think about it just yet. We want to enjoy the time we have together and worry about that later on."

"I would too," says Brian, "but at least leave it in the back of your mind."

Trevor nods in agreement. The pizzeria door opens, and he looks over to see a couple of families walking in and another group behind them.

Time for the lunch crowd. Ben's going to need help.

He stands up from the table and looks at Brian and Craig.

"I should get back to work. The lunch crowd is coming in." He points his thumb at the counter. "I'll see you guys around."

Trevor turns toward the counter, but Brian calls out to him, so he turns back to him.

"There will be a bonfire in a couple of days. You should come and bring Danielle. I'm bringing Lisa, and he's bringing Vicky. Everyone else will be there too."

He pauses for a moment. "I'll think about it and ask Danielle."

Brian and Craig nod as they say their good-byes. Trevor nods his head to them before turning around, and he walks around the counter to get back to work. Ben lets out a breath and is relieved when he sees Trevor behind the counter. He goes back to making pizzas while Trevor takes orders. He also debates whether or not he'll go to the bonfire.

17

BONFIRE

*T*revor jogs up the steps of Grandma Marie's porch. His day at the pizzeria is over, and he's doing as promised, spending time with Danielle and Jacob. He looks at the door and raises his hand up to knock. As he waits, he thinks back to what Brian and Craig told him. About the bonfire. He wants to go since he has spent little time with his friends this summer. And he's not blaming Danielle or her family. He loves spending time with them. It's just … it's the last summer he might see his friends. He'll ask Danielle if she would like to go with him.

He's in deep thought, so he doesn't notice the door opening and Grandma Marie trying to get his attention.

"Trevor?"

Trevor shakes his head to clear his thoughts and sees Grandma Marie staring at him. "Oh, hi! I was just thinking about something. Danielle and Jacob still home?"

"Of course." She nods. "Jacob couldn't stop talking about you coming."

He chuckles. "I've made an impression on him, I see."

"Young man, you've made an impression on this entire family," says Grandma Marie before she moves to the side. "Come on in."

"Thank you."

He walks in. Grandma Marie closes the door behind them and turns to face him. She motions toward the living room, and he nods before walking there. His eyes light up when he sees Danielle, sitting on the couch, watching Jacob play with his Nintendo Switch.

"Looks like you two are having fun."

Danielle looks at Trevor as Jacob stops playing his game.

"You're here!"

"Of course I am," says Trevor as he walks over and sits down next to Danielle, giving her a kiss on her cheek. He looks at Jacob. "I told you I would come over when I was done."

"True," says Jacob. "So, what are we going to do?"

"How 'bout we stay here today?" Trevor glances to Danielle and then looks back at Jacob. "We can play some games on your Switch or something. I'm beat from work."

"Fiiiine," Jacob sighs but jumps up as he remembers something. "I have a new game up in my room. I'm going to go get it, and we can play that!"

"All right. Sounds good! Go get it."

Jacob nods his head before running out of the room, and Trevor turns to Danielle, who smirks with a shake of her head.

"What?"

She grabs her phone.

You have him wrapped around your finger, and vice versa. It's cute.

"What can I say? Kids love me, especially that one," says Trevor. "How are you today?"

Good. How was work today?

"It was good. I had a couple friends come visit. Brian and Craig."

I heard. Jacob and my grandma mentioned something about them.
You've never talked about them before.

"There was nothing to mention." He shrugs his shoulders. "I didn't expect to see them much this summer since I was going to be busy working and they planned to get a head start in their college futures, but I guess things changed, and they came to find me. The last I saw them was at graduation, and we were all going our separate ways."

So, we didn't keep you from hanging out with your friends?

"Is that what you're worried about?" Trevor turns toward her as he rests his hand on her knee, and she shrugs her shoulders. "Elle, you didn't keep me from them. I hang out with you 'cause I want to. Even if I knew they were still around, I would have most likely chosen you and your brother 'cause I've had more fun with you guys than anyone else."

Really?

"Really." He nods before he leans in and presses his lips to hers for a slow, gentle kiss, and he pulls back with a smile. "Are you done worrying?"

Danielle nods.

"Good 'cause there's no reason for you to be worrying, silly girl." He chuckles as he leans in for another gentle kiss before speaking again, "Oh, and before I forget, I have something to ask you. Would you like to go to a bonfire? Brian and Craig, plus other friends of mine, are doing one and asked if I would go. And they want you to come too."

You want me to go with you and meet your friends?

"Yes," says Trevor. "It would be awesome for you to meet my friends. The guys are bringing their girlfriends, so you won't be the only girl. But it's okay if you don't want to. We can do something else."

Danielle looks at him, puzzled.

You wouldn't go without me?

"Nah. It wouldn't be as fun without you."

You can, you know. They are your friends.

"I know, but it'd feel weird without you there. You'd be all I thought about all night anyway." He smirks as he strokes her cheek with his thumb. "Are you saying you don't want to go? It's okay. I don't want you to be uncomfortable."

I'll go. It would be nice to meet your friends and to spend time with people around our own age. I love my brother, but you know ...

"Great." He chuckles. "And before you start wondering how you will communicate with them—"

She opens her mouth in surprise.

"Don't give me that look. I know you. You're going to over think everything and worry every second about not being able to socialize."

He moves his hand down to stroke her jaw before he continues, "You can bring your phone, a notebook, or anything that'll make you comfortable. Brian and Craig already know, and they understand." He leans his forehead against hers. "Promise me that from now up to the bonfire, you won't worry about it."

She looks him straight in the eyes and mouths, *Promise*.

"Good." He looks around the room to notice Jacob's not back yet and looks back at Danielle with a smirk. "Now, let's see how long we can do this before we get interrupted."

Danielle stares at him, confused, until she sees the smirk. He moves his hand up and runs the pad of his thumb over her lips before he leans in. She closes her eyes and rests her hand on his knee as she leans toward Trevor. But as their lips are about to touch, footsteps can be heard coming down the stairs. Danielle pulls away and opens her eyes to see disappointment all over Trevor's face. She giggles.

"Well, that didn't take long." He leans away and turns to see Jacob running into the room.

"I found it!"

ON SATURDAY NIGHT, Trevor sits in the driver's seat of his car as he drives down a road. He glances to his passenger seat to find Danielle staring out the window, thinking. He takes his right hand off the steering wheel and moves it over to her lap. He grabs her hand and laces their fingers together. Danielle lowers her eyes to their hands and then looks at him.

"Don't be nervous." He peeks at her. "My friends will like you."

She shakes her head and shrugs her shoulders, trying to reassure him that she's not nervous, but he doesn't believe it for one second. He gives her a *yeah, right* expression and gives her hand a tiny squeeze.

He continues to drive for a few more minutes before he makes a left turn into a parking lot. He drives around the lot until he finds an empty spot and pulls in. He moves his hand to his key to turn the car off. He takes off his seat belt and then faces Danielle.

"You okay?"

She looks at him and nods, giving him a small smile.

"Remember what I said. There is no reason to be nervous." He reaches for her hand again and squeezes it. "Also, at any point, if you want to leave, we can. I don't want you to feel like you have to be here just 'cause I am. Okay?"

Danielle nods giving him a bigger smile before she lets his hand go and takes her seat belt off. She reaches down for her bag and moves her right hand over to the door, but Trevor touches her shoulder, shaking his head.

"Let me get that for you," says Trevor before he opens his own door and steps out. After closing it, he jogs around the front of the car to open Danielle's door, and he holds his hand out. "Now, my beautiful lady, you may come out."

She giggles, shaking her head before taking his hand, and steps out of the car. He leans over and kisses her cheek before closing the door, locking it with his key. He puts the keys in his pocket and turns to his right. After lacing their fingers together, he pulls her close to his side, and they make their way to the beach.

As they reach the sand, they can see smoke in the air and follow it with their eyes to see the large bonfire in the center of the beach. Danielle looks up at Trevor with a grin. He grins back at her and leans down to capture her lips with his for a loving kiss. She pulls back and nods her head at the bonfire, and he nods. They walk toward the bonfire to find a group of people sitting on towels, talking and laughing.

"Hey, guys," says Trevor.

Everyone turns to them.

"Dude, you came!" exclaims Brian as he jumps up and walks over to them, giving Trevor a man hug. He pulls back. "No one thought you would show."

"Well, here I am." Trevor shakes his head with a laugh. He feels Danielle tightening her grip on his hand, and he glances at her before looking at Brian. "Brian, this is my girlfriend, Danielle. Elle, this is one of my best friends since elementary school, Brian."

Brian grins as he puts his hand out. "It's nice to meet the girl who has kept our boy here busy."

Danielle shyly smiles as she shakes his hand. He pulls his hand back. Trevor smiles as he gives her hand a squeeze.

"Well, T, why don't you go introduce your pretty girlfriend to everyone, and we can get this party started?"

"Dude, how many energy drinks have you had?" Trevor laughs and lets go of Danielle's hand, resting his hand on her lower back before moving her over to the rest of the group. "Elle, this is Craig, Lisa, Vicky, Will, Lynne, Dylan, Michelle, Elijah, and, Christina. You've already met Bianca. Guys, this is my girlfriend, Danielle."

"First, it's about time we saw you again, Trevor. We thought graduation was the last time we'd see you since you were planning to dedicate this summer to working," says Lisa as she giggles. She stands up as she grins at Danielle. "Second, it's very nice to meet you. Bianca told us about you after you two met, and she was right; you are very pretty."

Danielle blushes as she mouths, *Thank you.*

Elijah looks at Trevor and asks, "How'd you two meet?"

"I'm surprised Brian and Craig didn't tell you."

"Oh … I made Brian tell me, and Craig told Vicky, but I don't think they told anyone else." Lisa shrugs her shoulders as she looks over at Brian and Craig. "Did you?"

Craig shakes his head as he speaks, "We thought maybe you wouldn't want everyone to know or that you would want to tell them. We didn't know."

"It's fine," says Trevor. "Long story short, we met on the beach when I bumped into her."

Christina grins. "The whole run-in type thing, huh? That's sweet."

"All right, enough of this mushy stuff. I don't think Danielle is comfortable with this talk about them between everyone," says Dylan as he looks at her. "Are you?"

Danielle shrugs her shoulders, not knowing what to do or not liking all the attention being on her. Trevor looks at her with concern in his eyes and she looks up, shaking her head, reassuring him she's fine. He wraps his arm around her waist, pulls her close to his side, and gives her a peck on her temple. All the girls, minus Bianca, coo, and the boys smirk.

Trevor rolls his eyes as he turns to everyone. "What kind of food and drinks do we have here? I'm hungry, and I'm sure Danielle here is too, as she probably hasn't eaten much today, being so nervous to meet you crazy people."

"We have a barbeque set up on the other side, and we've already started making burgers and hot dogs." Will points at the other side of the bonfire. "And for drinks, we have sodas and juice. We decided that we would be on our best behavior tonight, so no alcohol."

"That's a first." Trevor laughs and looks at Danielle. "You want something?"

She nods, and before Trevor can say anything, Vicky walks up to Danielle, looping their arms together. "Don't worry, lover boy. I can bring her to the food. She'll be taken care of."

"Right," says Trevor as he keeps staring at Danielle. "You going to be okay?"

She nods.

"And you have your phone with you, right?"

Danielle nods again, patting her purse.

Christina walks over and pushes Trevor away from them as she loops her arm with Danielle's other one. "Great. The girls are gonna stick together, and don't worry, Danielle; we have a bunch of embarrassing stories about your boyfriend."

"Oh brother ..."

Danielle giggles. The three girls turn their heads and start walking away from the group. Lynne, Lisa, Michelle, and Bianca laugh before standing up and following them. Trevor and the guys watch them, and Trevor shakes his head, hoping the girls will look out for Danielle. He doesn't want her to regret coming.

Brian pats Trevor on his back. "Dude, she will be fine."

AFTER GRABBING THEIR FOOD, the girls walk over to sit down on towels that are set up next to the bonfire. Danielle decided to have a cheeseburger with a bag of chips and a bottle of lemon-lime soda. She takes a bite of her burger and gazes out at the water.

"So, Danielle," says Vicky after taking a bite of her own burger, "you and Trevor met at the beginning of the summer?"

Danielle nods.

"Is this going to be a summer fling, or are you planning to continue it after the summer?" asks Bianca after wiping her mouth with a napkin. "I mean … I don't know where you're going to school, but Trev has always talked about going to Stanford since we've all known each other."

All the girls, except Danielle, glare at Bianca. She looks at them and rolls her eyes as she shrugs her shoulders before looking back at Danielle.

Danielle puts her plate on the towel she's sitting on before taking her phone out.

I'm going to Harvard, and he's told me about Stanford. We're taking it day by day, and we'll see where things go.

"That's smart," says Lisa after sending another glare in Bianca's direction before looking at Danielle. "Brian told me you have a little brother. How old is he?"

He's seven.

"Aw, cute," says Lisa with a smile. "Are you two close?"

You wouldn't think we would be because of the age difference, but he's smart and mature for his age, so we're definitely close.

"I wish my siblings and I were that close," says Lynne with a sigh, "but we live all over the country. I'm the youngest and last one to go to college."

Michelle shrugs her shoulders. "I'm an only child."

Christina nods. "I have a younger brother, and he's like the devil's child."

They all laugh as they continue to eat their food. The guys, who are getting their own food, turn their heads to look over at the group of girls. Trevor looks at Danielle and smiles.

"See, man. I told you she'd be fine." Brian nudges Trevor with his elbow.

"I know, but ya never know," says Trevor as he shrugs his shoulders. "I've just been overprotective ever since what went down with Mark and Ray. She's also been hesitant around new people."

Craig nods. "I don't blame her."

"Brian and Craig told us about what happened." Will grabs a napkin and looks at Trevor. "That was low. Even for them."

"I remember when they used to be cool in elementary and middle school," says Dylan. "What the hell happened to them?"

"They grew egos," says Elijah as he shrugs his shoulders and takes a bite of food. "Who knows? I'm glad no one in this group went to the dark side with them."

Trevor nods in agreement.

BIANCA AND CHRISTINA stand near the edge of the water with their shoes off. Danielle and the other girls continue to laugh next to the bonfire. Bianca can't help but glance over at them with a somber expression. Christina notices.

"What's wrong?"

"I don't know." Bianca shrugs and stares out at the water. "It's just ... how can everyone easily accept Danielle like that? I mean ... I want to like her but ..."

"You can't because she's dating Trevor," says Christina, finishing the sentence, "and you still have feelings for him. And you wonder what would've happened if you two had never broken up."

Bianca looks at her in astonishment. "How'd you know?"

"Because everyone can tell, except Trevor since he's with

Danielle," says Christina, "and also how you kinda gave her the cold shoulder with the whole *what do you think will happen after the summer* question. I mean … way not to be obvious."

"I didn't mean to sound like that!" Bianca sighs. "I want him to be happy, and it seems he is, but how can he be? She doesn't use her voice. It must get kind of annoying when the other person doesn't speak or you don't know the sound of her … their voice. It also seems like he's annoyed over being so protective of her or something. I don't know. Wouldn't you get annoyed if you had to always ask the other person if they were okay?"

"Whoa, okay. First … breathe." Christina uses her hands to motion breathing movements, and Bianca rolls her eyes. "And second, it doesn't seem to bother him to be protective. To me, it looked like she's the one who's tired of him asking. But wouldn't you be like that for someone after what they'd gone through? I mean … Mark and Ray assaulted her."

"I know; I know." Bianca throws her head back and then gazes out at the water. "Which makes me feel a lot worse for feeling like I do. I just … I wish that were still me. The one he's protecting, hugging, holding hands with, and such."

"I know, but you're the one who broke up with him. He deserves to be happy, and he's happy with her," explains Christina. "And, B, you do this every time one of your ex-boyfriends starts dating someone new."

"Once again, I know!" Bianca throws her hands up. "But something is different this time. He's not like those other guys."

"And you should've thought of that last year," says Christina as she touches Bianca's shoulder. "He's happy. She's happy. You'll find someone who will make you happy again. Give it time. We're only eighteen."

Bianca nods as she continues to watch the water. Christina tells her she's going back by the bonfire and touches her shoulder again before turning around and walking back to everyone. Bianca crosses her arms. She turns her head to see her friends and Danielle laughing. She looks at the guys and sees them laughing. Each person now has someone, except her. She feels like she doesn't belong.

She looks at Trevor and wonders what could've been if they'd never broken up. They were happy together, but she wanted to move on. Why? She doesn't remember. She watches him look over at the group of girls, Danielle in particular, and he grins. His eyes brighten. As Danielle looks at him, he winks before turning away, and she sees Danielle's pinkish cheeks.

"He's never looked at me that way," she whispers to herself and looks up at the sky. "Maybe I should talk to him."

"I THINK we should go spend time with our girls," says Dylan as he motions his head toward the other group. "I mean … it's great to hang out with you guys, but our group isn't the same without everyone together."

Trevor nods. "I agree."

Brian chuckles before shaking his head. "Of course you agree. You haven't spent more than ten minutes away from your girlfriend."

"Not true," says Trevor in defense. "For the past week, I've gone to work, and that's, like, five hours away from her each day, so ha!"

Craig, Dylan, Will, and Elijah laugh while Brian shakes his head. Trevor playfully winks at Brian before throwing his plate in the garbage. He walks over toward the girls. He smiles at them before sitting down behind Danielle, placing his legs on each side of her as he slides close to her. He rests his hands on her waist and pulls her back toward him, so she lays her back against his chest.

"Hey, beautiful."

Danielle grins up at him and touches his hands as he moves them to rest on her stomach.

"I hope these girls have welcomed you with open arms," says Trevor before pressing his lips to her forehead before looking at the other girls.

"Of course we have," says Lisa. "We love her. She's funny ,and she fits right in with us."

"I knew she would," he says and smirks down at Danielle. "So … should I say *I told you so?*"

She rolls her eyes before looking back at the other girls and shifts to get comfortable against Trevor. The girls laugh as the rest of the boys come over and join them. Trevor rests his chin on Danielle's shoulder, and she pecks his cheek.

Lynne coos, "Aw, you two are so cute!"

"If I knew you would give us guys a terrible name in the romance department," says Brian in a joking tone, "I wouldn't have invited you."

"Like that would help." Dylan shakes his head. "Trev has always been better with the romantic stuff than we ever were."

"Elijah is very good with romance too," says Christina as she loops her arm with Elijah. "Just last week, we ate dinner while watching the sunset, and then we went on a midnight stroll on the beach to look at the stars."

"Atta-boy," says Trevor as he high-fives Elijah.

Craig shakes his head and wraps his arm around Vicky's shoulders, pulling her close to him as he kisses her cheek. "I'm not that bad with the romance. Am I, babe?"

"I guess not." She shakes her head and looks at him. "But it would be nice if once in a while, you did something like Trevor or Elijah."

"See!" Brian shakes his head. "You're making it hard for the rest of us."

Trevor shrugs his shoulders as he runs his hands down to the bottom of Danielle's shirt and sneaks his fingers underneath to lightly touch her stomach. She smiles as she rests her head back against his shoulder, and he pecks her neck.

Dylan looks around, noticing someone is missing. "Hey. Where's Bianca?"

"Oh, she's over by the water," answers Christina. "She wasn't feeling well before, so she went over there to see if it would help."

Lynne glances at Christina, not believing her. She saw the conversation that Christina was having with Bianca before. They showed the same body language they had when all the girls discussed the breakup between Trevor and Bianca. Bianca isn't over him.

I don't get why she can't let him be happy. I mean ... she broke up with him.

Lynne shakes her head. She looks at Trevor and Danielle and smiles.

TREVOR STANDS by the grill and flips the burger patty he's making himself. He glances over to his group of friends, and smiles seeing Danielle's face lit up. *That's a good sign.* He's thrilled that she's getting along with his friends and she seems to be having a good time.

Trevor looks back at the grill, and as he presses the spatula on the hamburger patty, he senses someone by him. To his right, he sees Bianca standing there.

"Hey," says Trevor. "Are you feeling better?"

Bianca raises her eyebrow. "What do you mean?"

"Christina said you weren't feeling well before—that's why you stayed by the water."

"Oh …" She nods her head. "Yeah, I'm feeling better."

"Good. Can't have you getting sick on everyone." He chuckles before taking his patty off the grill and placing it on the hamburger bun. Then, he turns to Bianca. "Well, if you'll excuse me, I'm going back over there. You should come back if you're feeling better."

"I'll think about it." She nods her head, and Trevor starts to walk away but Bianca calls out to him, "Trevor … wait."

He turns around. "What's up?"

She bites her lower lip. "I was wondering if we could talk."

"Okay …" He nods and waits for her to continue. "Go ahead."

"I, um … was wondering if you remembered what happened between us."

"What do you …" he starts to ask but realizes what she's referring to. "You mean, in our relationship?"

She nods. "Yeah … we were doing fine, but then everything changed."

"You broke up with me." He raises his right eyebrow. "You're the one who said things weren't the same between us and that we would be better off as friends. And I agreed."

"Have you … have you ever wondered what would've been if we'd never broken up?"

"Stop." He holds his hand up. "You're not doing this."

"I'm not doing what?"

"This. Bringing up our past and asking me the what if question."

"It's just a question." Bianca shakes her head, not understanding his reaction. "I've been thinking about it for a while. Even before graduation. We had a plan. We were going to go to the same school together. I'm still going. We can be that couple again. That couple everyone wants to be. I made a mistake, breaking up with you."

"We had a plan." Trevor shakes his head. "You changed it. I agreed with you about being friends and still going to the same school together, but plans change. I don't even know if I'm still going to Stanford."

"Why? Over some girl you just met, who doesn't even speak?" Bianca crosses her arms and rolls her eyes. "It's not like you two can communicate well. Wow. Are you really going to be able to handle always having to read what she's saying?"

Trevor shakes his head and struggles to stay calm. "You don't know what she's been through. I enjoy reading what she writes 'cause I only see it. It's our own language." He smiles, thinking of that. "And our families get along. My parents love her. I love her little brother. You know nothing about our relationship, so don't stand in front of me, acting like you do."

"Trev—"

"Don't." He takes a breath. "Ya know, I thought your other ex-boyfriends were joking when they said you tried to go back to them after they moved on. How 'bout instead of living in the past, you move on and find a new boyfriend?"

"I just …" She sighs and looks him directly in his eyes. "I … love you, Trevor."

Trevor can't believe what he's hearing. He really thought Bianca's previous boyfriends were kidding when they warned him after she broke up with him. Even her friends tried to warn him. But he didn't listen.

And now, she's standing in front of me, claiming she loves me?

He can't help but scoff at the thought.

"No, you don't," he says. "You want to 'cause you're upset that I moved on. That it's possible for people to move on from you. And if I were to be honest, I thought I was in love with you when we were together, but"—he glances behind him at Danielle—"I was wrong."

Bianca's heart breaks when she follows his eyes. "You love her?"

"I do."

"I—"

"Don't." He sighs as he looks back at Bianca. "I knew it would be hard to be just friends. For you ... not me. But if you can't accept that I moved on and am happy with Elle, then I don't think you and I can be friends."

"If that's what you want, then I guess ... I can accept that," says Bianca as tears fill her eyes, and she looks around feeling uncomfortable. "Can you, um ... tell everyone that I'm still not feeling well and I headed home?"

"You don't have to leave just because we're not friends anymore," says Trevor, motioning his head toward the group. "They are still your friends."

"But I'll feel uncomfortable, and I don't wanna ruin yours or any of their night. I'm sorry, Trevor. I just ... I wanted you to know or at least talk about it."

"And you did, and I don't agree." He shrugs his shoulders. "I still hope you have fun at college and do a lot with your life."

"Thank you, and same to you."

Trevor awkwardly nods before turning around, and he walks over to the group. Bianca watches him with sad eyes. She gets it. He's moved on. She watches her friends all laugh and sighs to herself, knowing she messed up. She wraps her arms around herself and looks down before walking off the beach, heading home. She doesn't notice Trevor watching her.

Elijah sees Bianca walking away. "Where is she going?"

Trevor looks at them. "She said she still wasn't feeling well, so she was heading home. She wanted me to tell you she'll call you all later."

"Oh …" Vicky nods. "Okay."

He smiles slightly before biting into his burger and sits down next to Danielle. He feels soft lips on his cheek, and he looks to his right to see her smiling at him. His eyes light up as he gives her a smile as he continues to chew his food.

Danielle types into her phone and shows it to him.

Are you OK?

He places a kiss on her lips before pulling away. "Never better."

She puts her phone back on the towel. He wraps his arm around her waist, and she rests her head on his shoulder. Trevor looks down at her and then around to his friends. He stares at the bonfire, not letting the smile fall from his lips.

Never better.

18

ATTACK

*T*revor lies back against the couch and kicks his legs up onto the coffee table as he enjoys his day off from work. He rests his hands on his stomach. He has decided to use his day off as a day to himself, where he can think about things. Danielle. College. Summer. He closes his eyes. *What am I supposed to do? I want to make my parents happy, but what about me? What about Danielle? See, this is why I didn't want to meet someone this summer.*

He shakes his head. He's happy he did. He's happy he met Danielle. Summer would've been boring without her and Jacob. The corner of Trevor's lips curve up as he thinks about her. Her smile. Her giggle. Her bright eyes. Her shampoo smell of lavender.

And he's going to be living three thousand miles away from her. He doesn't think he could manage that. He can't take being away from her for even a day.

Trevor opens his eyes when he hears footsteps. He looks over to see his dad walking into the room. He sighs to himself. *There goes my alone time.*

"Hey, son," says Joe as he sits next to him.

He sighs to himself again. "Hey, Dad."

"Sorry. Did you want to be alone?"

"No, it's fine," says Trevor with a fake smile as he puts his legs down. "Just thinking."

Joe notices the smile on Trevor is a fake one, but he lets it go. They sit in silence for a few minutes until the house phone rings. Joe reaches for it.

"Hello … Oh, hi, Marie … Is Danielle okay?"

Trevor turns his head to stare at his dad. He gets worried when Joe glances at him with concerned eyes. *Something's wrong.* That's all Trevor thinks about. All other thoughts clear his mind and focus on one thing. *What's wrong?*

"We will be right there." Joe hangs up and looks at his son. "Danielle's in the hospital."

Trevor jumps up from the couch. "What happened?"

"She was at the beach when she got attacked," explains Joe before he stands up as Trevor runs out of the room. "Trevor, wait! I'll drive you!"

DANIELLE LIES on the hospital bed with tears streaming down her cheeks. She can't believe what happened to her. She wasn't doing anything wrong. She was taking a walk by herself, as she wanted a day to herself and her thoughts. But out of nowhere, two White guys, dressed all in black, came up from behind her and started beating her and calling her names. They smacked her, knocked her down, and kicked her a few times.

There were a few witnesses who ran to help her before it went too far. The attackers ran. The police and ambulance were called. The witnesses gave the police a description of them.

She shakes her head as she keeps replaying what happened. All she wants right now is to be wrapped in Trevor's arms, so she can feel safe. She knows that after this, he will never let her out of his sight, even when he's working, but at the moment, she doesn't care.

The hospital door opens slowly, and in walks Trevor. He closes the door behind him and turns to see his girlfriend all bruised up with tears running down her beautiful cheeks. His heart breaks at the scene, and anger rises throughout his body. He wants to kill the guys who did this to her. If the police don't find them, he and his friends will—that's a promise.

But right at this moment, all he can do is stare at the broken girl. *His* broken girl.

She looks over at him, wanting him to hold her, and she holds her arms out for him. He smiles and walks over to the bed. Danielle moves over to give him some room, and he carefully lies down next to her, wrapping his arms around her.

"How's my favorite girl?"

He kisses her head and strokes her hair.

She gazes up at him with fresh tears forming in her eyes.

He hates seeing her like this. It's killing him inside.

Why would anyone want to hurt her? Her of all people?

Trevor wipes tears away and kisses her tear-stained cheeks. "It's going to be okay. I will not let anyone hurt you again."

She looks down. There's someone else she could use right now. Her mom. She was always great at comforting her if anything bad happened. But Trevor's doing a good job at it.

JOHN ANGRILY PACES around the hospital waiting room. He can't believe this happened to her, his baby girl. He's angry, way beyond angry. He wants those guys found and in jail fast, and he'll press charges. He will do everything he can to make sure they get what they deserve—that's a promise.

"John … you need to sit down," says Grandma Marie in a worried tone. "The police are doing everything they can to find them."

"I know, but it's not enough," says John with tears in his eyes. "She could have died."

"But she didn't."

"She could have though!" He sighs as he shakes his head. "I've already lost one person, and we almost lost you. I can't stand going through this again."

"John," says Joe as he stands up, "I know we don't know what you're going through, but we understand how you're feeling. They're doing everything they can to find them, and they won't stop until they do."

John sighs, knowing that they're right. He slumps down into a chair and puts his head in his hands. It hurts him, knowing there's nothing he can do, except be there for her. *How am I ever going to be okay with her going away to college after this?*

Jacob sits in one of the corner chairs as he watches his dad. He knows what happened and doesn't understand why people have to be like that. He doesn't like seeing his big sister hurt all the time, and even though he's only seven, he knows that he has to protect her. He is her only brother. Plus, he knows he has help from Trevor and Keegan.

Together, they will make sure nothing else happens to Danielle.

19

BACK HOME

"Ya ready to head home today?" asks Trevor as he looks down at his girlfriend, who's now sitting in one of the hospital wheelchairs.

Danielle grins while nodding as she can't wait to get out of the hospital. Two days was way too long. She shifts her body but groans because she's still sore. The doctors said she would be sore for a while and to take it easy.

"Babe … don't push yourself," says Trevor as he kneels down in front of her, taking her hands and lacing their fingers together. "Remember what the doctors said."

She rolls her eyes. Trevor chuckles. He leans toward her and captures her lips with his for a sweet kiss. Danielle smiles against his lips as she releases their hands, so she can slide them up to rest on either side of his face. Trevor places his hands on her knees.

"Oh … gross!"

They pull away when they hear a whine coming from the door and turn to see Jacob covering his eyes.

"I thought we already talked about this!" He removes his hands and crosses his arms, groaning. "I don't wanna see you two kissing. It's disgusting."

Trevor and Danielle laugh before he backs away from her. She looks over at Jacob and opens her arms. Jacob runs over to her and carefully wraps his arms around her. He starts crying against her shoulder. He cries every time he sees her. He hates seeing her hurt.

Trevor rubs Jacob's back. "It's okay, buddy. She's going home today."

"I know," says Jacob as he backs away and wipes his eyes. "These are happy tears."

Danielle smiles as she thinks about going home. She *hates* hospitals. She knows she has plenty of people who will take excellent care of her at home. A part of her is nervous about going home. *What if after I get healthy, everyone wants me to leave the house?* Her attackers are still out there, and she has an idea that they're not done with her, or they could be hurting someone else right now.

Trevor notices her looking into space. "Hey … what are you thinking about?"

She looks at him and shakes her head. She fakes a smile and hopes he doesn't see right through it. But she's wrong since he's been getting better at reading her and he can do so anytime and anyplace.

"Elle … what's wrong?" Trevor places his fingers under her chin and connects their eyes. "I know something is bothering you. What's up?"

Danielle sighs as she grabs her phone off the bed.

It's nothing. Just thinking about how happy I am to go home.

"Are you sure?"

She nods. She looks at Jacob, who shakes his head. He knows there's something else going on but says nothing. All three look at each other with soft smiles, knowing that in a half hour, Danielle will be home and away from the hospital.

DANIELLE LOOKS AROUND and smiles as she slowly sits down on her bed. She lets her hands hang on to the edge, and she glides her hands along the comforter. Her grandma's house feels more and more like home than her own house. She carefully scoots back and lies down, resting her head on her pillow. She puts her hands on her stomach and looks over to see Trevor leaning in the doorway with his arms folded.

He smirks. "Enjoying yourself?"

She nods.

He walks over and lies down next to her. Then, he rolls over, so he's facing her. "You seem like you've never been so happy to feel that bed under you."

She slowly pushes herself, so she can face him and nods.

"I don't think I told you, but"—he lifts his hand up and strokes her cheek with the pad of his thumb—"I was scared when my dad got the call from your grandma that you were in the hospital." He takes a breath as he runs his eyes over her face. "I don't know what I would've done if anything had happened to you. I … care about you so much. You have no idea."

He almost said it. He really did. The L-word was at the tip of his tongue, but he knows neither one of them is ready to say it. He knows they both feel it. But until she's ready to actually say it, he will keep it to himself.

She can read his eyes. She sees it. She senses it. He loves her. But he won't say it. And she understands why. He's not sure if she'll say it back. She wants to. She wants to open her mouth and let the words flow out, but there's still something holding her back.

Trevor leans forward and pecks her lips. "Now, missy … you need to rest, so you can leave the house again with me and enjoy the lovely outdoors."

Danielle giggles. But deep down, she knows it'll take a lot to get her to leave the house again since her attackers are still out there. She looks at Trevor and knows he would understand, just like how he understands her not speaking, but a part of her believes it won't be the same. He will want to go out. The summer is almost over, which means their relationship is likely almost over. She doesn't want it to be. But long-distance might not work.

"Hey." Trevor sees the faraway stare in her eyes. "We still have a few weeks left. Don't worry about it. We will talk about it when the time comes, okay?"

She bites her lower lip and nods but feels lips on hers. She doesn't respond right away, but then she closes her eyes and starts kissing back while putting her hand behind his head. Trevor rests his hand on her waist as he carefully leans over her, making sure he doesn't hurt her. She pushes closer to him as she deepens the kiss.

He grunts, as he needs air, and pulls away. He lies back on his pillow and looks at Danielle, whose eyes stay closed. He reaches out to touch her lips with his thumb. She opens her eyes and kisses his thumb before resting her head on his chest. Trevor wraps his arm around her waist and rubs her back while he puts his other hand on her arm.

They both wish they could stay like this forever and forget everything else. He knows she's hurting, not just physically, but also mentally. He doesn't know what will happen if the two guys aren't caught or when summer ends. But what he knows is, he doesn't want to say good-bye. She's his first true love, and even though it's early in either of their lives, she's *the one*.

20

TRIAL

his is not how Trevor and Danielle wanted to spend one of their last days together. But the time has come for the trial for Mark and Ray. Danielle doesn't understand how she's going to testify without speaking, but Trevor, her dad, and the prosecutor all assured her she would be able to use a notebook. That helped, but she's still nervous.

Trevor walks into Danielle's room, wearing a suit. "Are you ready?"

Danielle turns around. She smiles when she runs her eyes up and down. *He looks good in a suit.* She stares at him with a glint in her eye as she nods.

He grins, knowing she was checking him out. He holds his hand out for her, and she accepts it. Then, he pulls her close to him.

"How are you feeling?"

She gives him a thumbs-up. He looks her in the eye to make sure she's not lying. And she's not. She is better than she was. The bruises are gone. Yes, she's sore here and there when she moves the wrong way, but overall, the physical pain is gone. Mental, however, is a different story, but maybe the trial will somewhat help.

Trevor smiles and pecks her lips before they walk out of the room. They make their way down the stairs to join Grandma Marie, her dad, Jacob, and Trevor's parents in the living room. Everyone is going for support, as Danielle, Jacob, and Trevor will be testifying.

THE TALL BAILIFF looks out toward the crowd in the court room as he says, "All rise. Court is now in session, the Honorable Judge Andrews presiding."

Judge Andrews, a middle-aged man with gray hair, walks in and takes a seat.

The bailiff speaks again, "You may now be seated."

Everyone takes a seat and waits as Judge Andrews reads over the case. He looks over at Mark and Ray, not surprised at all to see them. He's always the judge for their cases and the one who put them on probation.

"Good morning, ladies and gentlemen." Judge Andrews looks around the court room before reading his papers again. "Calling the case of People of the State of New Jersey versus Mark Johnson and Ray Gills. Are both sides ready?"

Mr. Anderson, the prosecutor, nods his head. "The People are ready, Your Honor."

The defense attorney agrees. "Ready for the defense, Your Honor."

Judge Andrews looks at the bailiff. "Will you please swear in the jury?"

Danielle watches as the bailiff swears in the jury. She holds her hands together as her stomach is tied up by multiple knots. Trevor glances at her and moves his left hand over to her hands. He makes her hands separate as he laces their fingers. She looks at him, and he gives her a reassuring smile while giving her hand a slight squeeze.

The defense attorney sits down after giving his opening statement.

Judge Andrews looks at Mr. Anderson. "Is the prosecution ready to give their opening statement?"

Mr. Anderson adjusts his suit before standing up. "Yes, Your Honor."

"YOUR HONOR, I would like to call Trevor Williams up to the stand," says Mr. Anderson.

"Very well," says Judge Andrews, and he looks at Trevor. "Mr. Williams."

Trevor kisses Danielle's cheek and gives her hand a squeeze before standing up. He walks out from the bench and over to the stand. He stays standing as the bailiff walks over. He asks Trevor to raise his right hand.

"Do you solemnly swear to tell the truth, the whole truth, and nothing but the truth?"

"I do," says Trevor before he's asked to sit down.

Mr. Anderson stands in front of his desk as he asks, "Mr. Williams, you and the defendants have known each other prior to the incidents of this summer, correct?"

"Yes, sir."

"May I ask, how?"

"We've gone to school together since elementary school," explains Trevor, "but we were never close. Especially after a couple years ago when there was a hit-and-run accident in town and no one knew who did it. But I overheard Mark and Ray"—he glances over toward them—"talking about it. About them being the drivers, so I turned them in."

"Very well." Mr. Anderson nods before asking his next question, "Now … can you explain to us what happened that day at the pizzeria?"

Trevor looks at Danielle and then back to Mr. Anderson. "I wanted my girlfriend, Danielle, to come spend the day at work with me instead of hanging out around the house. I asked my boss, and he agreed. We started having fun with the flour, making a huge mess, and we were sitting on the floor, talking. Then, we started to kiss …"

Danielle's cheeks redden as she thinks about that day and looks down. Her family and Trevor's parents laugh at her embarrassment.

"But we were interrupted when we heard someone clearing their throat. We looked up to see Mark and Ray smirking at us. They started saying stuff to get a reaction out of us. Out of me. I told them to leave. Next thing I know, Mark grabs on to Danielle and pulls her up to him. He tried to make a move on her …"

Trevor stops for a moment and takes a breath to control his anger before he continues, "I stood up and pulled her away from him and behind me. Mark and I argued, which led to us fighting. Then, from the corner of my eye, I could see Danielle was pushed up against the wall with Ray on her. He started touching her, and she was uncomfortable. I got mad and punched Mark before stopping Ray. My boss came and called the police."

Mr. Anderson nods. "So … what you are saying is … they were harassing Miss Washington, even to a point where it could fall under sexual harassment?"

"Yes. And it wasn't the first time."

"When was the first time?"

"I-I think Jacob, Danielle's little brother, can tell you better than I can. I showed up at the end to stop them, but he was there the whole time."

"Very well. No further questions, Your Honor," says Mr. Anderson before he walks back to his table and sits down, lacing his hands together.

"Does the defense have any further questions for this witness?" Judge Andrews looks at the defense table, and the attorney shakes his head. "Mr. Williams, you may step down."

Trevor nods before standing up and steps down from the stand. He walks over and sits back down next to Danielle. He grabs her hand and intertwines their fingers as he leans over and whispers soothing words in her ear.

"The prosecution may call their next witness."

"With his father's consent," says Mr. Anderson, "I would like to call Jacob Washington up to the stand."

John nods. "I give my full consent for Jacob to speak on the stand if he wishes to do so."

Jacob stands up and quietly says, "I will speak."

"Very well," says Judge Andrews as he looks at Jacob. "Will you please step up onto the stand, where Mr. Williams was just sitting, young man?"

Jacob nods and walks up to the stand.

DANIELLE TAKES a breath as the current witness is dismissed. There's only one more witness left for the prosecution team. And she's it. It's now or never. She twiddles with her thumbs, as she's nervous. Nervous that people will either make fun of her or criticize her because she doesn't speak. Trevor rubs her back.

Mr. Anderson walks over and smiles softly. "Danielle, they're ready for you."

Trevor kisses her temple and whispers in her ear, "Everything's going to be okay. Just look at me, and you'll be fine."

She nods and stands, letting go of Trevor's hand. She walks out from the bench and over to the stand. The bailiff swears her in. She nods at the *I do* part and sits down.

Mr. Anderson walks over in front of the stand. "All right, Danielle, I will make this as simple as I can for you. I'll start with asking yes or no questions, and all you have to do is nod or shake your head, okay?"

She nods, and he begins.

"Do you remember the defendants pushing your brother down?"

She nods. She glances at Mark and Ray, only to see them glaring at her. She moves her eyes away from them and back to Mr. Anderson.

"Were you afraid they would do something to you that day?"

Danielle nods as tears form in her eyes. Trevor sees the tears, and he shifts forward in his chair, letting his elbows lean against his knees. He's doing everything in his power not to run up there and comfort her because he knows he can't without being thrown out.

"Was everything that Mr. Williams and Jacob said here true? About the first time you ran into the defendants and at the pizzeria?"

She nods.

"Is it also true that about a week ago, a couple weeks after their arrest, two guys attacked you when you were walking around town?"

A tear falls down her cheek as she nods again. Mr. Anderson reaches into his pocket and takes out a handkerchief, handing it over to her so she can wipe her eyes.

"Do you believe that Mr. Johnson and Mr. Gills were somehow involved or were the ones who planned the attack?"

Danielle bites her lower lip as she looks at Trevor, his parents, and her parents before looking at Mark and Ray. Mark's the only one glaring at her while Ray has his head down. She closes her eyes. Then, she nods her head before reopening her eyes.

Mr. Anderson walks over to his desk to grab a pad and pen before walking back over to the stand to hand them to Danielle. "Can you write to me why you think it involved them?"

She takes the pad and pen. She starts writing, leaving Trevor and everyone else confused, except Mr. Anderson. Danielle looks up at him and hands the pad back to him. He reads it over and smiles, placing his hand on her shoulder.

"You're doing well," says Mr. Anderson. "While I read this … would you like Trevor to be up here with you?"

Danielle nods.

"Okay." He takes his hand off her shoulder and looks at Judge Andrews. "Your Honor, I would like to ask the court's permission for Mr. Williams to join Miss Washington on the stand to comfort her while I read what she wrote to the jury."

The defense attorney stands up. "Objection!"

Mr. Anderson shakes his head. "Your Honor, what I have to read is sensitive for our witness to hear out loud. She's not the one on trial here—they are—and if she needs someone up here to be with her, then I think that should be allowed."

"I agree," says Judge Andrews before looking at the defense attorney. "Overruled." He looks at Trevor and motions with his finger for him to come forward. "Mr. Williams, you are welcome to join Miss Washington on the stand."

The defense attorney shakes his head as he plops back down in his chair. Trevor jumps up from his seat and walks out from the bench, trying to control himself as he walks over to Danielle. The bailiff puts another chair in the stand for Trevor. The moment he sits down, she wraps her arms around him and clings on to him. He wraps his arm around her and rubs her back while he rests his other hand on her arm before kissing her head. Everyone in the courtroom smiles and coos.

"Okay. I had Miss Washington write why she thought the defendants were involved in her attack last week," says Mr. Anderson as he shows the notebook to the jury and courtroom, "and here is what she wrote.

"When I was being beaten down and kicked, the two guys were yelling at me that I was a worthless piece of shit and that it was no wonder why Mark and Ray had them do this. One of them said, 'Too bad they aren't here; this would've been hella more fun.' That's how I figured it was Mark and Ray who had put them up to it. And I didn't tell anyone because I was scared they would come back and finish what they'd started."

Everyone looks at Danielle, who now has tears streaming down her cheeks. While he's trying to calm her, Trevor glares at Mark and Ray. Judge Andrews looks around the room and over at Danielle. He's never done this before, but he's heard enough. He doesn't want to waste anyone's time. He looks over at the jury and can see they all have similar expressions while staring at the young couple.

"Mr. Williams and Miss Washington, will you please step down from the stand and return to your seats?" asks Judge Andrews.

Trevor looks at him, confused, but nods. He stands up with Danielle in his arms, and they walk from the stand over to their seats. Danielle sits down, and her dad leans over to give her a big hug. as he, too, has tears in his eyes.

How could this have happened to my baby girl? He figured it was bad but not that bad.

He releases her and lets her fall back into Trevor's arms. John smiles softly as he watches them. He's happy that she found someone like Trevor.

"Mr. Anderson, please take a seat," says Judge Andrews. Then, he looks around the courtroom before continuing, "Okay, this is not conventional, but I think we've heard enough today. The Court is prepared to proceed to verdict and sentencing."

The defense attorney's eyes widen as he stands up. "But, Your Honor … my clients have not been given the opportunity to defend themselves!"

"Counsel." Judge Andrews stares at the defense attorney and points at him to sit. "Your clients have been in my courtroom countless times. And I remember clearly stating last time, if they ended up back here, I wasn't going to take it easy on them. So, here it goes."

He looks down at his paperwork and scribbles some notes as he figures out the verdicts and sentencing before looking back up. "Mr. Johnson and Mr. Gills, please stand."

They stand.

"You two are found guilty of the following charges: probation violation, endangering the welfare of others, assault, and emotional damages," says Judge Andrews. He looks at Ray. "Mr. Gills, you are also found guilty of sexual assault."

They look down.

"Mr. Johnson, I am sentencing you to ten years in state prison," says Judge Andrews, "and, Mr. Gills, I am sentencing you to twenty years in state prison."

Gasps can be heard throughout the courtroom. Danielle wipes her eyes as she sits up to listen to the judge. Trevor smiles softly as he rubs her back. *Finally, the losers are going away.* He looks over at them and can't help but smirk at their shocked expressions.

"And it could be longer if," says Judge Andrews as he looks at Mark and Ray, "you don't give us the names of the guys you paid to attack Miss Washington. Are we clear?"

They nod their heads and then look back down, knowing they messed up this time. Judge Andrews motions his head at the two officers who are standing near the exit.

"Get them out of the courtroom," says Judge Andrews as he hits his gavel on his desk.

The officers nod and walk over to quickly handcuff Mark and Ray. They escort them out of the room. Trevor, Danielle, and their families watch as they leave, relieved that it went in their favor. The courtroom is then dismissed.

Danielle takes deep breaths as she lets herself calm down. Everyone is concerned for her, but they know she will get through this.

WHEN THEY WALK into Grandma Marie's house, Danielle goes right up the stairs to her room. Everyone watches her, feeling somewhat helpless. Today was the first time they found out that Mark and Ray had had something to do with the attack. Grandma Marie and John guessed that while she talked to Mr. Anderson, preparing for the case, he got her to open up.

Jacob is the first person to break the silence. "Is she gonna be okay?"

"Would you like me to check on her?" asks Trevor.

John nods. "Yes. She will probably only want you."

Trevor nods in agreement before running up the stairs. He takes a deep breath as he stands in front of her door. He loosens his tie from around his neck before knocking on the door. He knows she won't answer the door, so he pushes the door open to find her on her bed, sobbing. His heart breaks again.

"Ya know … this is becoming a routine," he jokes, trying to lighten the mood but gets a glare back from her. "Right. No time for jokes."

He walks over to her bed and kneels down beside it, reaching for her hand. He rests his other hand on her cheek and uses the pad of his thumb to wipe her tears away. She looks at him. He smiles before leaning in and brushes his lips on hers before pulling back. She pulls her arms close to her as she gives him a slight smile.

Trevor reaches for her phone and rests it on her bed. "Will you type to me?"

Danielle stares at the phone. She sighs and then looks up at him to see his pleading eyes. She grabs the phone before sitting up and sliding over, so Trevor can sit next to her. He puts his arm around her, so she feels protected as she types.

What do you want to know?

He looks at it and then at her. "Why didn't you tell anyone you thought they were involved?"

I was scared. Nervous.

She stops for a second before continuing.

I just … wanted it to go away and have everyone forget about it. If I told you, there would've been more problems, and I didn't want that.

I just wanted to enjoy summer.

Trevor reads it. He takes the phone from her hands and puts it on the bed on the other side of him. Then, he shifts, so he's leaning toward Danielle before placing his hand on her face to turn her, so she's facing him. He strokes her skin.

"There is nothing that will ruin the rest of this summer. We're going to enjoy it together. And I want you to tell me whatever is going on in that beautiful mind of yours," he says as he continues to stroke her face. "I'm not letting you go through this alone."

She smiles. He leans in to give her a passionate kiss, and then he lowers her down to lie on her back as they continue moving their lips together. They both know that the next few weeks are going to be the best weeks of the summer. Because they're leaving the drama behind.

At least, they hope so.

21

BIRTHDAY SURPRISE

*D*anielle lies on her side on her bed as she watches *Gilmore Girls* for the millionth time. She decided today would be a lazy day, as she's still trying to get past the court trial and memories of the attack. As she's watching the episode where Rory leaves her grandparents' house after staying there for a few months, her cell phone makes a dinging sound.

She grabs her phone off her end table and looks at it with a smile, noticing it's a text from Trevor.

Trevor: *Good afternoon, my darling.*

Danielle giggles as she touches her phone to open the keyboard.

Danielle: *Darling? Where did that come from? LOL. Good afternoon to you too, sir.*

After pressing Send, she puts the phone on her bed in front of her, and she looks back at the TV. Not even a minute later, another ding can be heard, so she picks it back up and engages in a lengthy conversation with Trevor.

Trevor: *Honestly ... IDK. I just added that. Who knows? LOL. How are u doing?*

Danielle: *Interesting ... LOL. And I'm good. Just relaxing and enjoying a lazy day today. Trying to forget all the troubles of the summer, so I can enjoy the rest.*

Trevor: *That's good. Everyone deserves one. Hope I'm not a part of the troubles. ;)*

Danielle: *Nah, not anymore. ;) LOL. What are you doing today? How was work?*

Trevor: *What do u mean, not anymore? Know something I don't know? :P Eh, work was work. BTW, I hear your grandma is bringing Jacob over here to play in the game room while she and Mom do women things.*

Danielle: *IDK. Is there something I should know? :P LOL. Yes, Jacob has been bugging us to bring him back to your house. Grandma said she wanted to talk to your mom about something. You don't know what it's about?*

Trevor: *Why would I? My mom doesn't tell me anything. So, if they're going to be here, why isn't my beautiful girlfriend coming with them?*

Danielle: *I told you. It's a lazy day, and I'm dedicating it to Gilmore Girls.*

Trevor: *Ah, Gilmore Girls ... your favorite show.*

Danielle: *That it is.*

Danielle looks at her phone and thinks the conversation just ended. But she knows better. He'll find something else to talk about. If she wasn't so lazy, she would have gone over to Trevor's house with her grandma and Jacob, but they agreed that everyone needs a lazy day once in a while, so this is hers.

As she rests her head against her arm and pillow while watching *Gilmore Girls*, another ding is heard. She rolls her eyes. She was right. He wasn't finished.

Trevor: *So ... 2morrow is a big day.*

Danielle: *I guess ...*

Trevor: *You guess? You only turn 18 once. And 2morrow's the day one of the most beautiful girls in the world turns 18.*

Danielle: *One of? LOL.*

Trevor: *Well, you have my mom, my aunts, cousins, my grandmas, your grandma. So, yes, one of. But between you & me, you're number one. And don't change the subject. Tomorrow's your birthday!*

Danielle: *Your secret is safe with me ... LOL. I wasn't trying to change the subject! But, yes ... 2morrow is my bday ...*

Trevor: *You don't sound thrilled. Come on, baby! It's your bday!*

Danielle: *I'm excited. It's just hard. It's the first one without my mom.*

Trevor: *Shit. I didn't think of that. I'm sorry. :(*

Danielle: *It's okay. Plus ... I don't think I have anything planned for 2morrow.*

Trevor: *Oh, please. Like I'm going to let you not have plans. It's your first bday without your mom, but I will make sure you still have the best bday ever!*

Danielle: *Oh ... what are we doing then?*

Trevor: *Well, first, we're having a late lunch at the restaurant where we had our first date, and then we'll see how the rest of the day goes.*

Danielle: *You're planning something, aren't you?*

Trevor: *IDK what you're talking about. Elle, I'm going to let u have fun on your lazy day. Your brother just arrived, and I'm sure I won't have much time to text.*

Danielle: *Okay. Have fun and don't lose too much. :P*

Trevor: *I'll have you know, I won that game we played at your house the other day.*

Danielle: *Oh, I'm sure you did. Go have fun.*

Trevor: *I will. Enjoy your Gilmore Girls marathon.*

Danielle: *Thank you.*

Danielle smiles and shakes her head, knowing he's planning something. He would. And it's not like she doesn't want to celebrate. She just wishes her mom were here with them.

Not letting herself get into too much thought, she reaches over to put her phone back on the end table. She then sits up and scoots, so she's leaning against her headboard, pulling the blanket over her legs. She rests her arms on top of the blanket as she stares at the TV to continue her marathon.

Trevor smiles as he slides his phone into his back pocket. He turns to face the other three people in the room, who are looking at papers while sitting around the dining room table.

"Are you done texting my sister?" asks Jacob.

"Yeah."

Sarah looks up from the papers. "Does she have any idea?"

"She suspects something, but I don't think she's one hundred percent sure."

Grandma Marie smiles and looks at Sarah. "I can't thank you enough for helping me put this surprise party together for Dani. It means a lot, and it'll mean a lot to her."

"It's the least I can do," says Sarah as she pats Grandma Marie's hand. "After everything she's been through, she deserves a party that will be all about positivity and her."

"I agree! Because she's the best big sister, and she deserves the best!" exclaims Jacob with a grin. "So, what's the plan again?"

Grandma Marie, Sarah, and Jacob face Trevor.

"Well, first, I'm going to take her to the restaurant at the hotel around three. Then, you three, Dad, and John will set up the banquet hall right down the hall, and guests should start showing up about four thirty. I'll bring her there about five, five fifteen."

"Sounds good," says Sarah. "And who are the guests going to be?"

"I invited Keegan and his parents, my friends—minus Bianca—Danielle's friend Britney and her parents. Plus, Britney's bringing a few of her friends. Also, some of Marie's and John's friends, a few people from the hotel, neighbors, and a couple other people."

"I think that's a good amount of people," says Grandma Marie as she nods. "And we have some food coming from the pizzeria as well as from the hotel, right?"

"Right."

"Great. We have the plan," says Jacob. Then, he jumps up. "It's time for me to beat you!"

"Sure, kid." Trevor shakes his head and chuckles. "I'd like to see you try."

Jacob jumps up and down, waiting impatiently for Trevor to stand up. Trevor pushes himself up, and they walk out of the room, pushing each other. Grandma Marie and Sarah watch them, shaking their heads as they laugh.

Grandma Marie then looks at Sarah.

"What do you think will happen when summer ends?"

"I don't know," says Sarah. "I'm hoping they'll make it work. I've been meaning to talk to Joe about giving Trevor another option for school. Maybe he could go to Harvard instead if he wants. I wasn't always on board with pushing him toward Stanford"—she shrugs her shoulders—"and now, I'm really not. But the talk will have to wait until after the party."

Grandma Marie nods in agreement. "Your son brought something back to Danielle that I haven't seen since my daughter-in-law passed. And I don't know what would happen if things didn't work out between them. I don't think she'd be able to handle another heartbreak."

They nod to each other before looking over the plans for the party.

"HAPPY, HAPPY BIRTHDAY!"

Danielle's eyes open, and she groans as she brings her arm to her eyes to block the light of her room. She closes her eyes but senses movement on her bed. She flutters her eyes back open to see Jacob jumping up and down. She shakes her head and laughs.

"You're eighteen years old!" Jacob grins as he stops jumping and plops down onto his knees next to her. "How do you feel? Any older? Like an adult?"

Danielle holds her hand out to stop Jacob from continuing. She laughs as she sits up in her bed. She stretches her arms and yawns before sitting back against the headboard. Then, she grabs her phone.

First, thank you. I feel the same as I did yesterday. No, I don't feel any older or like an adult yet.

"Oh, well, maybe you will." He shrugs his shoulders. "Do you want breakfast? Grandma told me to come wake you up 'cause she wants to make a special breakfast for your birthday, but she wasn't sure what you would be in the mood for."

I'll come down. Let me go to the bathroom first.

Jacob nods excitedly as Danielle pushes her comforter off her and gets up from her bed. As she stands, she stretches her arms out and then down before shuffling Jacob's hair. She walks toward her connected bathroom and goes in, closing the door behind her.

He watches her and then jumps off her bed, running out of the room and down the stairs. He goes into the kitchen to see his grandma and dad sitting at the table.

"She's in the bathroom. She'll be down when she's done."

Grandma Marie nods. "Thank you, Jacob."

John whispers, "Mom, is everything set for tonight?"

"Yes," answers Grandma Marie in a whisper. "We will leave here right after Trevor picks up Danielle for their early dinner."

John nods his head before looking down at the table to read the newspaper. He reaches his hand out to the coffee mug next to the paper and picks it up, bringing it to his lips. As he takes the sip, he sees Danielle walking into the room with her phone in hand. He puts the mug down and lets go of the newspaper. John pushes his chair back before standing up, and he goes over to wrap his arms around Danielle.

"Happy birthday, baby girl."

She returns the hug, and his lips press to the top of her head before she pulls back.

She mouths, *Thank you* to him.

Grandma Marie stands up and steps over to wrap her own arms around Danielle, wishing her a happy birthday.

As Grandma Marie pulls back, she leaves her hands on Danielle's upper arms. "Now, honey, what would you like for your birthday breakfast?"

Danielle shrugs her shoulders as she sits down at the kitchen table with her phone.

Anything would be fine.

"Nonsense," says Grandma Marie as she shakes her head and puts her hand on Danielle's shoulder. "It's your birthday. You deserve a great breakfast. Anything you want."

I guess I'll have chocolate chip pancakes with whipped cream and strawberries on top. Also, some powdered sugar. I mean, only if you have everything to make that. If not, I can just have regular pancakes.

"Again, nonsense," says Grandma Marie. "I went shopping yesterday before we came home from Trevor's house and bought everything that could make those. I thought you'd want them. Jacob and John, would you like some chocolate chip pancakes as well?"

Jacob and John nod. Grandma Marie smiles before walking over to the refrigerator to take out eggs, butter, and milk. Then, she puts them on the counter before grabbing sugar, flour, baking powder, salt, and chocolate chips out from the lower cabinets. As she makes the pancakes, Danielle reaches out for the apple juice container that's on the table and grabs a cup, pouring the juice in it before taking a sip.

"So, baby girl"—John looks at Danielle—"what would you like to do today?"

Trevor is taking me out for a late lunch, early dinner thing.

"That's nice," he says with a knowing smile. "Want to do anything before?"

Danielle shrugs her shoulders.

Jacob speaks up, "She'll probably take *forever* to get ready for the thing with Trevor anyway, so doing anything before is out."

She gasps at Jacob and playfully pushes him as she giggles.

"What?" Jacob shrugs. "It's true. But we can do presents when she gets home!"

Danielle moves her eyes from Jacob to her dad with confusion and shakes her head.

You didn't have to get me anything.

John nods. "Of course we did. It's your birthday, and you only turn eighteen once."

Jacob exclaims, "And you'll see them tonight!"

She smiles as she nods her head. She looks down at the table as she bites her lower lip. John notices the sadness in her eyes. He sighs, knowing what she's thinking about, and he places his hand over hers.

"Dani … I know you're thinking about your mom. She would want to be here with you for your birthday, but she would also want you to be happy today. Before she passed, she told me she wanted me to make sure you still enjoyed your birthdays—especially the big ones, like this one—so please, for your mom, can you enjoy today?"

She looks up at her dad with tears in her eyes but nods as she lets the corners of her lips curve up. John smiles before standing up and walks over to her, bending down to wrap his arms around her, giving her a tight hug. He presses his lips to the top of her head before sitting back down on his chair.

Grandma Marie smiles and places a stack of pancakes on a plate. She grabs the whipped cream, strawberries, and powdered sugar before walking over to the table. She puts everything on it. "I thought you all would enjoy topping your own pancakes. I know each of you is particular about your pancakes. Anyone want syrup?"

They shake their heads. John and Jacob voice their thank-yous as Danielle mouths hers. Danielle reaches for a plate and starts grabbing a couple of pancakes. She then puts powdered sugar on top, followed by whipped cream and a couple of strawberries. Grandma Marie sits down at the table as John and Jacob work on their breakfast. They all look at each other before nodding with smiles and start eating.

As Danielle chews her pancakes, she looks at her dad, knowing that he was right. Her mom would want her to be happy. *I'm going to enjoy the day. Just how she would want me to.* She looks back at her plate, sticks her fork into the pancakes, and continues eating her delicious breakfast.

DANIELLE LOOKS at herself in the mirror as she applies lip gloss to her lips, finishing the last of her makeup. She smiles and nods in approval before putting her makeup away. She turns toward the door to check herself out in the wall mirror. She's wearing a sparkly blue blouse that sits above her hips and a pair of black dress pants. She finishes her outfit with a pair of black pointed-toe pumps. *Perfect.*

The doorbell rings, and she looks at the mirror for one more moment before opening the door to walk out of the bathroom. She grabs her purse off her bed and walks out of her room, and then she heads down the stairs. As she reaches the middle of the stairway, she sees Trevor standing by the door, laughing with Jacob and her grandma.

Dad must be somewhere else in the house.

She smiles as she continues down the rest of the stairs. When she reaches the bottom, she notices what he's wearing—black jacket over a white shirt with nice black slacks and shoes. *Handsome.*

Trevor can sense eyes on him, so he looks over to see Danielle standing there. He stops laughing and lets his eyes run over her.

"Ah, there's the birthday girl," says Trevor as he walks over to her and leans forward to give her a sweet kiss. "Happy birthday, Elle. You look beautiful."

She blushes as she mouths, *Thank you.*

"Ready to go?"

She nods but looks around, wanting to say bye to her dad but doesn't see him.

Grandma Marie notices this, so she says, "Oh, your dad went to run a quick errand at the store. He wanted me to tell you to have fun and enjoy your lunch slash dinner."

Danielle smiles and then looks at Trevor, nodding. He takes her left hand with his right hand, interlacing their fingers together. She gives Grandma Marie a one-armed hug, and Grandma Marie kisses her cheek. Jacob also gives Danielle a hug before Trevor opens the door. He releases their hands, so Danielle can walk out first. Before he follows her, he turns to wink at Jacob and Grandma Marie.

Plan is a go.

They nod. Trevor grins as he pulls the door closed. He turns around to see Danielle staring at him. He pecks her lips before grabbing her hand. They walk down the front steps toward his car. Trevor opens the passenger door. Danielle smiles gratefully as she gets in. As she puts her seat belt on, Trevor closes the door and runs around to get in on the other side.

"Ready for an awesome birthday meal?"

She nods. Trevor puts his seat belt on, and before starting the car, he grabs Danielle's hand to kiss the back of it. He then rests her hand on his thigh before he puts the key in the ignition and turns it. He looks in the mirrors before he pulls away from the curb.

THE DOORMAN HOLDS the door open for Trevor and Danielle. Trevor nods to the man who has been working at the hotel for as long as he can remember. As they walk into the hotel, Danielle smiles as she gazes around. It's just as beautiful as she remembered. She then feels Trevor's fingers interlacing with hers as he leads her toward the restaurant.

"Ah, Mr. Williams and Miss Washington, welcome back!" Mr. Davidson says enthusiastically. "I have a table set up for the two of you. The same one from last time you were here. Is that all right, Mr. Williams?"

"Excellent, sir."

"Great. Follow me," says Mr. Davidson as he grabs two menus before turning around, walking over to a table that's set up for two with a candle in the middle. "Here you go."

Trevor smiles as he pulls a chair back for Danielle. She smiles and sits down on the chair. He pushes it in just enough. Danielle puts her purse down as she gazes around. Trevor walks around the table to sit down on his own chair.

Mr. Davidson smiles. *His parents raised him right.*

He puts one menu down in front of Danielle and one in front of Trevor.

"I hope you enjoy your afternoon," says Mr. Davidson, and he looks at Danielle. "Oh, and I hope you have a great birthday, Miss Washington."

She smiles at him, and Mr. Davidson walks away. Then, she

stares at Trevor with her right eyebrow raised, and he shrugs, holding his hands up.

"He didn't hear it from me. My dad must have told him or maybe even your dad. Who knows?"

She giggles and shakes her head. *Sure … like I believe that.* She reaches into her purse to take out her phone, resting it on the table.

Danielle looks at the menu on the table and picks it up, opening it, and she thinks about what she's going to order. Trevor chuckles as he watches her. She glances up from the menu and gives him a *what* expression. He shakes his head before picking up his own menu.

A young man wearing a black shirt and pants, holding a pitcher of water in one hand and two glass cups in the other hand, walks over, placing the cups on the table. Then, he fills them up with water. "Welcome to the Sand Castle Restaurant here at the Crystal Waves Hotel and Resort. My name is Wade, and I'll be your waiter today. What can I get you to start off with? Drinks?"

"Thank you, Wade," says Trevor. "I'll have a cola, and she'll have a lemon-lime soda. We would also like to start with the sampler appetizer."

"Great. I will put the order in for your appetizer and come right back with your drinks."

Trevor nods as Wade walks away and chuckles as he turns to Danielle. "Must be new."

Danielle looks at him, confused, and reaches for the phone.

How do you know?

"One, he didn't greet me with my last name ,which most do. Two, he did the whole welcome speech, and I've mentioned to the other workers that they don't have to be too formal with me," says

Trevor, shrugging. "So, that means they haven't had time to tell him."

She nods. Wade walks back over with their drinks in hand. He puts the lemon-lime soda in front of Danielle while he puts the cola in front of Trevor. Then, he reaches his right hand into his shirt pocket for two wrapped straws. He puts them on the table before taking out his pad.

"Your appetizer should be out soon," says Wade. "Are you ready to order, or do you still need some time?"

"I'm ready. Are you, Elle?"

Danielle nods as she types her order and slides it over to Trevor, who reads it and then looks at Wade. "She will have the chicken francese over linguine while I'll have the veal francese over linguine. Can I also get a side order of meatballs?"

"Um … I'll have to check with the chef and manager if we can do that, but I'm sure there won't be an issue." Wade nods his head. "Anything else?"

Trevor tries to hide the smirk that forms along his lips but fails. "Yes. Can you ask Tyler Bryant, one of the sous-chefs, how much the bet is and who's part of it?"

"What bet, sir? And you know Tyler?"

"I do. You can ask him how while you get my answers from him. Thank you."

"Right away," says Wade with a confused tone in his voice. "I'll be right back with your answers as well as with your sampler."

"Thank you."

Wade walks away, and Trevor can't help but laugh.

Then, he turns back to Danielle. "I forgot to mention that some-times, the workers here tend to bet on how long it'll take the new guy to learn who the bosses are."

She reaches across the table for her phone.

I'm learning a lot about this place on my bday.

"What can I say? It's been a while since a new server served me. It's fun."

She giggles while shaking her head. She reaches for her drink and brings it up to her lips just as she sees Wade coming through the kitchen door. He's carrying a plate of food. She looks back at Trevor and motions her head toward Wade.

"This should be interesting."

"Um … I have your sampler," Wade says as he puts the plate of food in the center of the table. He glances behind him at the kitchen doors to see the man nodding his head, so he turns back to Trevor. "And, sir, Mr. Williams, Tyler wanted me to let you know that everyone's in on the bet. Even Mr. Davidson. Tyler also said for you to stop ruining the fun. Mr. Davidson won the bet since he knew you'd do exactly what you did."

"Wonderful." Trevor chuckles. "I'm sorry for putting you through that. I don't get why they tend to do that to the newbies. I sometimes enjoy it. But I have to say, you're very good at your job. Next time when you see me, you don't have to do the lengthy introduction to me."

"Thank you, Mr. Williams," says Wade with a sigh of relief. "I hope you two enjoy your appetizer. I will be back with the rest of your meal shortly."

Trevor nods.

Wade turns away and glares at the kitchen doors before going to another table.

Trevor looks at the kitchen doors to see Tyler standing there, shaking his head, mouthing, *You suck,* at him before laughing and going back into the kitchen.

Trevor laughs before looking at the sampler and then at Danielle.

"Ready to start your yummy birthday meal?"

Danielle nods excitedly before grabbing one of each to put on her plate.

JOHN, Jacob, Grandma Marie, Joe and Sarah are in the banquet room of the hotel, setting it up for the party. Grandma Marie and Sarah are working on the light-red table cloths and placing the chairs around the tables. John and Joe are putting up the balloons around the room. Jacob puts a couple of presents on a large table that will be dedicated as the present table.

Joe looks at John. "Do you think she'll be surprised?"

"My mom said that Trevor mentioned she was curious yesterday," says John as he shrugs his shoulders while tying up a balloon. "But I think she'll still be surprised, especially for that big present your son is keeping from all of us."

"Yes! I don't know what it could be." Joe shrugs his shoulders. "So … I know we've talked recently about your job position for after the summer since you and Jacob will be going back up to Skystead—"

"I've been meaning to talk to you about that," John interrupts him. "I think we're going to move down here. We have a lot of memories, and I think Jacob would do better, around my mom. We love our town, and I'm planning on keeping the house in case we go back, but for now, I think Calm Beach is the answer."

"That's a big decision," says Joe. "Have you told Jacob or Danielle?"

"We talked about it last week before the trial," says John. "I was

169

worried about how Dani would feel, but she agreed. Jacob jumped in excitement. My mom said we can continue living with her, and I think it'd be good for Jacob and me to be down here. Dani will be away at Harvard for most of the next four years."

"Well then, I guess I don't need to worry about losing my manager." Joe chuckles and pats John on his back. "Welcome to the neighborhood."

TREVOR WIPES his mouth with his cloth napkin before resting it on the table and then sits back in his chair, holding his hands on his stomach. "That was delicious."

Danielle nods in agreement as she takes one more bite of her chicken before placing the fork onto the plate. She pushes the plate away as she grabs her napkin off her lap and wipes her mouth before tossing it onto the table. She reaches for her drink and brings it up to her lips to take a sip, and then she puts it on the table.

Wade walks over and smiles, noticing the empty plates. "How were your meals?"

Danielle puts her right thumb up, and Trevor chuckles.

"Very good. I think we'll be ready for the check in about five minutes."

"Your dad already took care of it," says Wade as he takes the empty plates off the table. "Mr. Davidson told me after the secret bet was out. Your dad also covered my tip, so no need to worry about that either. I hope you both have a great rest of the evening."

"Thanks, Wade." Trevor nods as Wade walks away, and he looks at Danielle. "Do you need to sit for a little, or are you ready to go now? I'm in no rush."

Danielle narrows her eyes as she types.

Why? Do u need to get me somewhere?

He shakes his head. "I don't know what you're talking about."

Uh-huh, sure. I'm ready to go.

Trevor grins as he pushes his chair back and then stands up. He walks over to Danielle's side and holds out his hand. She puts her hand in his. He pulls her up. He leans in to press his lips to hers for a loving kiss before pulling away.

They walk away from their table and toward the entrance, where Mr. Davidson is standing. "I hope you enjoyed your meals, and have a great rest of the evening."

"Thank you, Mr. Davidson," says Trevor as he shakes his hand.

The two of them walk out of the restaurant. Just as Danielle takes steps toward the front doors, Trevor shakes his head and leads her the other way. She stares at him, confused. He smiles and gives her a look of reassurance as he interlaces their fingers. They continue to walk through the lobby. He then takes a left down another hallway and then stops in front of a door.

He glances at Danielle. "Earlier, my dad asked me if I could check on this room while we were here. You can come in with me."

Danielle tries hard to give him a serious look, but she can't stop the corners of her lips going up. She's secretly shaking her head. *He's not very good at keeping a surprise, but he's cute, trying. I'll let him have his fun.*

She nods. He smiles before reaching for the knob and pulls the door open.

She walks in first and sees the room filled with people who yell out, "Surprise!"

They all clap as Danielle's mouth widens in surprise. She looks around to see balloons everywhere, signs that have *Happy Birthday, Danielle* written on them, a table full of presents, and many people standing around.

She might not have been surprised for the actual party, but to see just how many people are there is what surprises her—Trevor's friends, Keegan and his parents, Britney and her parents, Trevor's parents, some of her grandma's neighbors, her grandma, her dad, and Jacob. She also sees people she doesn't recognize.

"Happy birthday, little angel!" exclaims Keegan as he walks up, giving Danielle a hug.

She rolls her eyes at his nickname before pulling back, giving him a smile. He shakes Trevor's hand as she walks around, greeting everyone. They each hug her and wish her a happy birthday and ask how she's doing. After making her rounds, she sits down at one of the empty tables.

Britney walks over and plops down next to her. "How ya doing, birthday girl?"

Danielle nods with a smile as she takes her phone back out.

Good. Full though. Their food here at the restaurant is AMAZING!

"I know. Mr. Williams was setting up a buffet for dinner. I kinda snuck a peek." Britney giggles as Danielle shakes her head, laughing. "Oh, and Trevor's friends are cool. We were talking before. I brought some of my friends, and apparently, we have mutual friends."

You went to different schools?

"Yeah, we're not from the same area." Britney shrugs her shoulders. "Hey. I heard you got your orientation letter for Harvard! I did too! Maybe we'll run into each other."

That's awesome! At least we'll know each other. It's crazy that we're a couple weeks away from starting our college lives.

"I know! I'm nervous but excited," says Britney. Then, she glances at Trevor, who's sipping a drink while talking to his friends, and she looks back at Danielle. "What's going to happen between you two? Brian told me Trevor's going to Stanford."

Danielle shrugs her shoulders. She looks at Trevor, sighing, knowing their summer is ending, and so could their relationship. She doesn't want to think about that. Not now. Britney notices the change in her mood and shakes her head, putting her hand over Danielle's.

"Sorry. Didn't mean to bring your mood down," says Britney. "You don't need to be thinking about that today." She then jumps up from her chair. "Come on. Let's go mingle and get your mind off what's coming."

Britney puts her hands on her chair and looks down at Danielle before motioning her head toward everyone else. Danielle glances at them, nodding as she grabs her phone. She stands up, and they walk over to the group that includes Trevor, his friends, and Britney's friends.

"Danielle! I can't believe you didn't tell us your birthday was during the summer!" exclaims Lisa as she shakes her head. "I would've thrown you a gigantic bonfire party at the beach." She puts her hand on Trevor's shoulder. "Not that this isn't a *great* party, but mine would've been bigger and better."

"Well, my girlfriend isn't huge on extravaganzas, so," says

Trevor as he pushes Lisa's hand off his shoulder, "no. Mine is better. Especially since I invited people she actually knows. And you would've invited everyone in Calm Beach."

"But ..."

Brian shakes his head and puts his arm around Lisa's shoulders. "Babe, you know he's right. I love you, but you do take parties and make them extreme."

"Ugh, whatever," says Lisa as she shakes her head and then looks at Danielle. "How's your birthday so far? Having fun? Has our friend here"—she nods her head toward Trevor— "treated you well today?"

Danielle laughs, nodding her head.

> Yes. I'm having a great day. It started out with my adorable but annoying brother bouncing on my bed to wake me up.
> Then, I had a delicious breakfast and a wonderful dinner.

Vicky smiles. "As long as you're enjoying your day."

> I am.

"Good," says Trevor as he wraps his arm around her waist, pulling her close to him. He kisses her temple. "Then, we did something right today."

TWO HOURS LATER, everyone's finishing up the cookies-and-cream cake made by one of the local bakeries. Danielle is sitting at a table with Trevor, their friends, and Jacob. She wipes the cream off her lips with a napkin. She looks at Trevor when he laces their fingers together while their hands rest on the table.

He scoots his chair closer. "So, a little birdie told me your dad and Jacob, plus you when you're on breaks, are moving to Calm Beach."

She nods as she types.

Yeah. My dad likes his job and decided he wanted to live closer to Grandma. Jacob also loves it here. We're still keeping the house in Skystead, just in case we ever want to visit or move back.

"That's cool," says Trevor before pressing his lips to hers.

Danielle smiles against his lips. He's about to pull away, but she moves her hand behind his head, leaving it close to hers as their lips continue to move. She doesn't think about the other people in the room, just about Trevor and his lips. But they hear a throat being cleared. They pull away from each other and look around to see everyone staring at them; some are laughing while others are whistling. Danielle blushes as she hides her face in Trevor's chest. He chuckles as he kisses the top of her head, not letting her hand go.

"So, if we're all finished embarrassing my daughter," says John with a chuckle as he stands in front of the room with a small wrapped package in his hand, "I would like to say something. Trevor and I decided that even though she said we didn't have to get her anything, we would do something special for her anyway. As her father, I've earned the right to go first."

Trevor nods and salutes him as he chuckles. Danielle pulls away from Trevor's chest, confused, when she turns to face her dad.

"To begin, as many of you know, our family took a hard loss

before the summer. My wife of twenty years passed away after fighting cancer for a couple years." John smiles softly as he takes a breath. "She was so strong, and she fought as hard as she could. There were two important reasons she fought so hard, and they are our children, Danielle and Jacob."

John looks over at Danielle and Jacob with a slight smile. Danielle's eyes tear up. Trevor puts his right hand on her back and rubs it up and down as he puts his left hand on Jacob's shoulder, giving it a slight squeeze.

"My wife knew there was a chance she wouldn't be here with us to celebrate Danielle's eighteenth birthday, so one of the last things she requested from me was to give her the gift she would've given her," says John with tears in his eyes. "Dani, can you come up here, please?"

Trevor gives Danielle's waist a slight squeeze before she pushes her chair back. She takes a deep breath, and then she stands up and walks over to her dad.

"Sweetie, this is something your mom wanted you to have." John looks down at the box in his hand and then back at Danielle. "You know how much she would've loved to be here with you. She wanted me to give this to you on your actual birthday." He hands the box to her. "Remember to smile when you open it."

Danielle nods as a tear falls down her cheek, and she takes the box in her hands. John leans forward to kiss her cheek before stepping back to give her some space. She takes a breath and then starts taking the paper off. Once she gets it off, she hands the paper to her dad. She removes the lid of the box and places it on the bottom. She sees a small folded card and takes it out, opening to see her mom's handwriting.

Hi, Sweetheart.

If you're reading this, it means it's your 18th birthday!

Happy birthday, baby girl. I hope you're having a special one.

Remember, just because I'm not physically there with you, I am there with you in your heart. In this box is something that I hope will remind you of that. I love you, Ellie-Bear. I hope you enjoy this birthday and many more.

Love,
Mom ❤

Danielle takes a breath as she closes her eyes and moves her hand up to her face, wiping away the tears off her cheeks. After she dries her cheeks, she opens her eyes and moves the card to under the box as she holds it. She looks in the box and carefully moves tissue paper to find a heart locket necklace underneath. Danielle takes it out, holding it up.

She stares at her dad, who nods. She hands him the box to hold before she opens the locket. She notices two pictures. On the left side, there's a picture of her mom sitting in a rocking chair, holding her when she was a baby. On the right side, it's a family picture taken during the summer last year. Danielle smiles as she runs her finger over the pictures.

John steps forward. "Would you like me to put it on for you?"

Danielle nods and hands him the locket. He gives her the box to hold as he goes to stand behind her. He moves her hair out of the way as he puts the necklace around her neck. Danielle grabs a hold of the heart locket. After linking the necklace, John walks around to face her and kisses her cheek before taking the box from her, putting the card back inside and placing the lid back on top.

"Your mom would be proud that you listened to me about living your life." John chuckles. "All she ever wanted was for you and Jacob to be happy. Don't forget that."

Danielle nods with a slight smile. She brings her hand to her face again to wipe away the rest of her tears. John looks over at Trevor and nods his head at him. He then walks over and takes a seat at the table with Grandma Marie, Joe, and Sarah. Trevor smiles before standing up and walks over to where Danielle is standing. He puts his hands on her cheeks and strokes them with the pads of his thumbs.

He whispers, "You okay?"

She nods.

"Good. I'm hoping my part will put a happy smile on that beautiful face," says Trevor before he leans in and pecks her lips. Then, he turns toward everyone. "I don't know how I'm supposed to top that but here goes nothing." He chuckles. "I'm sure most of you know that Elle and I met this summer. And it's been one of the best summers because of her."

He glances at Danielle and smirks, noticing her cheeks turning pink.

"I've learned a lot about my beautiful girlfriend, and one thing is, she's a *huge* fan of *Gilmore Girls*. And when I say huge, I mean, huge. She spent her lazy day yesterday, having herself a *Gilmore Girls* marathon," says Trevor, "while I was finishing the planning for this party with my mom, Marie, and Jacob."

Danielle rolls her eyes at both him mentioning her lazy day and the fact that her grandma and Jacob went to his house to do more than just play games. She knew. Or at least, she thought that was what they were doing. And she was right.

"Well, everyone knew I had something more planned for her," says Trevor as he looks at Danielle, "and that's my present." He reaches his right hand into his back pocket and takes out an envelope, holding it out toward her. "I hope you like it."

She looks at him, curious, and then takes the envelope from his hands. She turns the envelope around to the opening side and tears it open. *I wonder what it is.* She reaches into it, takes out a piece of paper, and then unfolds it. She reads over the words and her eyes widen. *No way.* She stares at Trevor with her mouth agape.

She mouths, *Are you serious?*

He nods. Danielle tightly wraps her arms around his waist. He chuckles as he returns the hug and pulls her close to him. Danielle pulls away with a grin as she looks back at the paper and reads it over again.

"Now, that's the smile I want to see on your face. It's a good idea we went in the order we did." He chuckles as he watches her read over the letter before he turns to everyone else. "I just gave Elle a trip to meet the cast of *Gilmore Girls* and to take a tour of the set. The show's been off for a while, but I talked to one of the producers, and she said it's not an issue."

Danielle grins as she once again reads the letter from the producer inviting her plus a few guests whenever they're able to come. She also left an email address for Danielle to email for more information. She puts the letter back into the envelope and throws her arms around Trevor's neck, looking at him with bright eyes.

"Happy birthday, Elle."

She mouths, *Thank you.*

He grins and wraps his arms around her waist, letting his hands rest on her lower back so he can pull her against him. Danielle stands on her tippy-toes and presses her lips to his. Trevor smiles against her lips and closes his eyes as the kiss deepens. Neither cares who's watching. But they get interrupted when applause breaks out in the room, and the guys start whistling. Danielle pulls back, blushing, as Trevor kisses her cheek.

"You'd better text me when you get to Harvard," says Britney as she pulls back from the hug with Danielle. "Remember, if you need anything, I'll be there."

Danielle grins as she nods. Then, she watches Britney, her parents, and her friends leave the room. For the last half hour, she's been saying good-bye to the guests. Trevor's friends were the first ones to leave but not before they agreed to meet up before the summer ends.

Keegan grins as he walks up to Danielle.

"I still can't believe you're eighteen." He shakes his head. "My little cousin is not so little anymore. What am I ever going to do?"

She rolls her eyes as she watches his parents say bye to her dad, and she grabs her phone.

U still have Jacob to watch grow up.

"True." Keegan nods in agreement and then wraps his arms around Danielle. He kisses the top of her head. "Happy birthday, angel."

She smiles against his chest before they pull away from one another. They walk over to join her dad and his parents. Her uncle and aunt each take their time to give her a hug, again wishing her a happy birthday and good luck at school. Then, they turn around and walk out.

"Are you ready to head out?" John looks at Danielle, and she nods. "All right. Let's go say bye and get your grandma and Jacob."

She walks over to the table, where Grandma Marie, Joe, Sarah, Jacob, and Trevor are sitting, and Jacob sees them walking over.

He jumps up from his chair. "Are we leaving?"

"Yes," says John as everyone else stands up from their seats. "Thank you for helping us put this together. We really appreciate it."

"It was no problem," says Joe as he shakes John's hand. Then, he turns to Danielle. "I hope you had a wonderful birthday today."

She grins and nods. Joe gives her a small hug, followed by Sarah. As Grandma Marie and John say their good-byes, Trevor grabs Danielle's hand and pulls her away from them.

He turns to her and rests his left hand on her cheek as he places his other hand on her waist.

"I hope today was as much fun as it should have been for you."

She nods as she presses her phone against his chest, and Trevor watches her as he strokes her cheek lovingly.

I had a great time. Thank you. For everything. I know you're the one who started the planning. I couldn't have asked for a better day—other than wanting Mom here.
But in some way, she was. Thank you, Trevor.

"You don't have to thank me. I wanted you to have a day all 'bout you, so you could forget the negativity of the summer and focus on the positives." He smiles and pecks her lips. "I love seeing you smile, and I'll do anything to keep you smiling. I'm glad you had a great day, and you did very well, pretending to be surprised."

What? But I was surprised.

Trevor gives her a *come on* expression.

Okay, fine. But I was a little surprised. I mean, I had an idea, but I didn't think there would be that many people. It was more than I could have ever asked for.

"Well then, that's all that matters."

Trevor closes his eyes and leans down to captures her lips for a slow but passionate kiss. He pulls her against him, so there's no room between them. Danielle grunts against him as she moves her arm up to the back of his neck. He opens his mouth and licks her lower lip, asking for entrance and she gladly lets him in. But before he can explore her mouth, he remembers where they are and that they're not alone, so he reluctantly pulls away.

He rests his forehead against hers and whispers, "I don't want to say good-bye."

Danielle nods in agreement and makes enough space between them, so she can type.

We'll see each other tomorrow.

"But that's sooo long away." He pouts playfully and then sees Jacob, crossing his arms and staring at them. "Okay. No more playing around. Looks like your brother is ready to leave, and he's giving me that *get off my sister, I want to leave* look."

It's cute that you're so scared of my little brother.

"He can be very intimidating," says Trevor and Danielle laughs. "Hey. Don't laugh. I'm being serious!"

She sarcastically nods her head as she continues to laugh.

The adults walk over to them and Grandma Marie looks at Danielle. "What's so funny?"

"Nothing. Nothing at all." Trevor shakes his head and rolls his eyes at Danielle. "I said something and for some reason, she found it amusing."

John chuckles. "Well … we're heading out now."

"Okay." Trevor nods and looks at Danielle giving her a peck on the lips. "Text me when you get home?"

She nods.

"And I'll see you tomorrow, most likely after work. Sound good?"

Sounds good.

Danielle kisses Trevor's cheek after giving him a hug. She turns toward her family and gives Joe and Sarah a smile before taking steps toward the exit. Jacob gives a high five to Trevor before running after Danielle. Grandma Marie hugs Trevor. John gives him a hand-shake. They say their good-byes before following where Danielle and Jacob went off.

Joe pats Trevor on his back. "Great job, son."

Trevor smiles. "Thanks, Dad."

wo weeks. Two weeks until summer ends. Two weeks I have left with Danielle. Her birthday party marked the beginning of the last weeks of summer. I wish it didn't have to end. I wish our summer could last forever, but ... it has to come to an end. Everything does at one point, even when you don't want it to.

Sarah walks in the living room and sees her son lying on the couch as he stares up at the ceiling. "Sweetie ... are you okay?"

Trevor glances at her for a moment before staring back at the ceiling, not answering.

"Is it Danielle?" she asks, and Trevor nods his head. "Sweetie ... it doesn't have to end when summer ends. I can see how much you care for her. And love her. You can make a long-distance relationship work."

"Really, Mom?" asks Trevor in a slightly sarcastic tone as he sits ups. "How do you expect us to make it work when she doesn't speak, huh? Ever think of that?!"

Sarah understands his outburst. "There are other options."

"Like what? Texting, e-mail, video chat, and Facebook and other social media? Are those the options you're talking about?" he asks again sarcastically, and Sarah nods. "It won't be the same. I need to have her in my arms. I need to be able to comfort her if anything bad happens. I need to be there to protect her. And I need … I need to hear her voice."

"Sweetie …"

"I have to go," says Trevor as he stands up. "I'm meeting Danielle and Jacob."

He walks out without saying another word, leaving Sarah worried and concerned.

It's time to have that talk. She turns around and walks down the hall to her husband's office.

She knocks on the door until she hears, "Come in," from the inside.

She walks in.

"We need to talk."

JACOB HOLDS DANIELLE'S hand as they walk along the shoreline, waiting for Trevor. Jacob looks up at Danielle, knowing this will be a hard couple of weeks for her. She's just starting to get back to herself again, but once summer is over, he's scared she might turn back to the girl she was at the start of summer. He'll also miss Trevor when summer's over.

"Well, well, well, what are these two lovely people doing, walking all by themselves?" They hear a voice behind them, followed by a chuckle.

Jacob turns around. "Trevor!"

"Hey, little man," says Trevor as he turns around and crouches down. "Hop on."

Jacob grins and walks over. Then, he gets on Trevor's shoulders, resting his hands on Trevor's head. Trevor grabs his legs, and he stands up.

Danielle smiles at the two of them. She's happy they get along so great. But then again, it could end up being a terrible thing because it would mean she's not the only one who will get hurt in the end.

Trevor walks over to her. "Hey, what are you thinking about?"

Danielle shakes her head, not wanting to talk about it. He looks over her face and knows what's wrong. She's thinking the same thing he was before—not just about the two of them though, but also about Jacob.

He walks closer to her, taking one of his hands off Jacob's leg, and wraps his arm around Danielle, so he can pull her into his chest. She rests her head on his chest, trying to hold back the tears. Trevor pulls back and leans down to peck her lips. He moves his hand up to stroke her face and moves a strand of hair off her face.

"We're gonna find a way, okay?"

She nods.

"Now, put a smile on that beautiful face, and let's find something to do to keep our minds off what's coming, okay?"

She blushes at his *beautiful* comment. She'll never get used to his compliments. He grins. He loves making her blush. But most of all, he loves making her giggle. It sounds like an angel sent down from heaven. It also gives him hope that she's getting closer and closer to sharing the sound of her voice with him.

Hopefully soon. Then, maybe, just maybe, the long-distance thing could work.

But he also knows she might not, and he's not sure how much longer he can take it.

"So, what are we going to do?" asks Jacob as he looks at them with excitement.

Trevor loves when Jacob gets excited. He's like the little brother he's always wanted, and now, he has one. He doesn't want to lose him either. *This is why I told myself not to get too attached to anyone this summer!* But it's too late.

"Well … I was thinking we could go to the arcade down the street," he suggests but laughs when he looks up and sees Jacob's disapproving look. "There are a lot more games there than at my house."

"Then, let's go!" exclaims Jacob as he grabs on to Trevor's head and moves it to the side to show him he needs to start walking.

DANIELLE LAUGHS as she watches Trevor, running around trying to keep up with Jacob. He seems exhausted after playing with Jacob for almost two hours straight.

Trevor bends over with his hands on his knees and narrows his eyes at her. "Wh-what do you think is so funny, missy?"

She just shakes her head and continues to laugh. She sees Jacob coming back from the bathroom with new energy. She knows he will be this energetic for the rest of the day, and she can't help herself, so she turns around and laughs harder.

"What?" asks Trevor as Danielle points behind him. He glances back to see an energetic Jacob. "Oh no. Hide me!"

Trevor runs behind Danielle and tries to hide. Jacob runs over to Danielle and looks around, not seeing where Trevor is, so he looks at Danielle. She giggles and uses her thumb to point behind her. He grins as he walks around her and grabs Trevor's arm, dragging him away.

Trevor playfully glares back at Danielle and mouths to her, *You're gonna get it.*

TREVOR CRASHES DOWN on the couch. "I'm beat."

Danielle laughs as she walks into the living room with two cups of lemonade. She hands one to Trevor before sitting down next to him. He takes a sip and then puts the cup on the coffee table. He puts his arm up to rest on the couch.

"How's my favorite girl doing?"

She scoots closer to him and looks up at him. She then mouths, *Good.*

Trevor grins as he moves his arm down to wrap around her shoulders. "I'm glad. So, what do you want to do tomorrow?"

Danielle shrugs, but then an idea comes to mind, so she grabs her phone.

I just got an idea. Could you take me to the cemetery to visit my mom's grave? I mean … you don't have to, but I haven't been there since the day of her funeral.

"Sure," answers Trevor, "but isn't it back in Skystead?"

She shakes her head.

No. It's only a half hour from here. She wanted to be buried, near Calm Beach, where her parents were. She loved it down here.

He kisses her cheek. "We'll go first thing in the morning."

23

MEMORIES

*D*anielle stares out the window as Trevor drives through the grand entrance gates of the cemetery. She takes a deep breath. She senses the car pulling over and coming to a stop. She looks at Trevor as he turns the car off.

He looks at her.

"You okay?"

She nods but shrugs her shoulders at the same time, as she's unsure. He gives her a slight smile before taking the key out of the ignition, and takes his seat belt off. He pushes his door open and gets out. Then, he runs to her side to open her door. She closes her eyes for a second and takes a breath before opening them. Then, she takes her seat belt off and steps out of the car.

Trevor grabs her hand and laces their fingers together. "Do you remember where it is?"

Danielle bites her lower lip as she gazes around before shaking her head.

"Okay. We'll just walk."

She nods. Trevor locks his car, and they walk along the path while looking at the different gravestones. Danielle continues

189

biting her lower lip as she tries to remember where her mom's gravestone is. But she doesn't think she was focusing where they were driving or going when they were at the cemetery a few months ago.

"Daddy?" asked Jacob with sadness as he sat in the backseat. "Where are we going?"

"We're going to a place called a cemetery," explained John as he tried to hold his emotions back while following the hearse carrying his wife. "It's where your mom will be buried with Grandma and Grandpa."

"Mommy's going to be living in dirt?"

John sighed as he continued to explain, "Yes, and no. She will lie in the casket she was in at the funeral parlor though."

"Oh ... okay," said Jacob as he shrugged his shoulders, still confused. Then, he looked at Danielle. "Are you okay, Dani?"

Danielle looked back at him with a sad smile. She nodded before staring back out her window with tears in her eyes, not really paying any attention to where they were going or caring about anything that was happening around her.

"Elle ... I think I found it," says Trevor as he points at a headstone.

She looks over and sees a familiar rectangular grayish headstone. She nods. They walk over to stand in front of the headstone and read what's written on it.

IN LOVING MEMORY

OF

SANDY WASHINGTON

WIFE, MOTHER, DAUGHTER

LOVED BY MANY

MARCH 25, 1972—JUNE 20, 2019

Trevor lightly squeezes Danielle's fingers. "Would you like to be alone?"

She shakes her head before freeing her hand from his grip. Then, she sits down on the ground with her legs crossed. She looks up at Trevor and motions for him to sit with her. He smiles as he stands behind her and sits down. He scoots, so he can put his legs on either side of Danielle. She leans back against his chest, and he wraps his arms around her waist. She touches his hands and then closes her eyes as she thinks back to last summer.

"Mom," said Danielle as she looked at her mom sitting on the couch with a book in her hands, "can we go to the aquarium?"

"Sure, honey," said Sandy as she put her book down before standing up. She walked over to the staircase to yell up, "Jacob! We're going to the aquarium!"

Jacob excitedly ran down the stairs. He loved the aquarium. If he could, he'd spend every day exploring. But the best time of going to the aquarium was when he was with his family, especially his mom. Even at six years old, he knew this could be one of the last times that they could go there with her. And they would enjoy every second.

* * * * *

"Mommy!" exclaimed Jacob as he ran toward his mom and the man with her. Danielle was not that far behind him. "Bobcat is getting big!"

"I bet he is," said Sandy before leaning down to kiss his forehead. "Say hi to Keegan."

"Hey, little man," said Keegan before picking him up. "How you doin'?"

"I'm great!" exclaimed Jacob after being put back down on the floor.

Keegan smiled at Danielle. "And how's my baby angel doing?"

"I'm not a baby anymore, Keegan." Danielle rolled her eyes. Then, she

wrapped her arms around his waist as she spoke, "But I'm good. I've missed you."

"I know. I've been busy lately. It's what happens when you become an adult."

∽

DANIELLE LOOKED AROUND and found her mom sitting on a bench, using her key, scratching at it. She raised her eyebrow as she walked over. She sat down and watched her.

"Mom ... what are you doing?"

Sandy took a breath and looked at her. "Sweetie ... can you go get your brother for me? I want both of you to see this together."

"Okay." Danielle got up from the bench and walked around to find Jacob by Bobcat's tank. "Hey. Mom wants to show us something."

He nodded and took Danielle's hand. They walked back to the bench. Danielle stopped when she saw tears in her mom's eyes and had an idea of what was going on but would wait until her mom told them. Danielle didn't want the day to come. The day where she would make them promise to keep on living even though she wasn't. She wanted her mom to live longer. All the doctors had said she only had one more year, but it wasn't enough. Danielle took a breath before she and Jacob walked over and joined their mom on the bench.

"Kids ..." Sandy wiped her tears before she continued. "I asked Keegan if I could carve something on a bench." She turned to them. "And I chose this one because when you sit here, you can see many parts of the aquarium from this very spot."

Together, they looked around as they saw many tanks filled with multiple kinds of species and hallways that led them down to other areas of the aquarium.

Sandy said, "I want you kids to understand that even when I'm not here anymore, I'll always be with you."

Sandy pointed at the spot of the bench where she had been carving. Tears filled Danielle's eyes as she read the words that had been carved. She bit her lower lip to stop the sob that was threatening to come out. She wasn't ready.

It's not time yet. No. It's too soon.

"It says, No matter what happens … I'll always be watching over you," Sandy said out loud for Jacob, knowing he wasn't one hundred percent with reading yet. "And it's true. I will be there with you. When you need me, just look inside yourself, and I'll be there."

Danielle scooted closer to her mom and wrapped her arms around her. Tears fell down both their cheeks, and then Jacob joined in on the hug. They all knew. They knew this would be the last time they would be at this aquarium together. Because there was a big chance that Sandy Washington would not make it back next summer.

And they were right.

DANIELLE'S EYES are filled with tears as she continues to think back to that day. Trevor can tell she's fighting the emotions she's feeling. He tightens his hold on her as he looks down at her and kisses behind her ear. She opens her eyes and turns her head to look at him with red eyes.

He leans down, brushing his lips against hers, and then pulls back, resting his forehead against hers as he whispers, "She's watching over you right now. And I know she's smiling because you're happy. She wants you to be happy. I want you to be happy."

Without moving from her spot, Danielle reaches in her purse to take out her phone.

I think she would've liked you.

"I wish I'd gotten to meet her," says Trevor. "I would've thanked her for giving birth to the most beautiful and kindest girl in the world, who's going to be my girl for years to come."

More tears come to Danielle's eyes after he says that. She knows he means it, but she has a feeling that it won't be like this for long. The summer is ending. They're going to two different schools across the country. He will get tired of her not speaking. She knows her mom wants her to be happy and to find a way for them to work it out. But she can't think of a solution other than to start speaking, and for some reason, she's not ready.

Trevor kisses her tear stained cheek. "Are you ready to head back?"

She nods before crawling off him. He smiles as he pushes himself off the ground. He holds his hand out for Danielle to grab, and she accepts it. He pulls her up and close to him. He brushes his lips against hers. She pulls back and smiles. She looks at the stone one last time before she takes a step away. But Trevor doesn't move. He looks at the headstone.

"Mrs. Washington, I wanted to let you know that you have the most beautiful daughter in the world, and I'm honored to be her boyfriend. Thank you. Thank you for giving her life and raising her to be the best girl she is." Trevor smiles at Danielle and kisses the back of her hand. "Now … we can go."

24

LAST DATE

*D*anielle looks at herself in the mirror. She lets her hair down as she finishes getting ready for what could be her *last* date with Trevor. She has a gut feeling that it is. The last one. She hopes it's not, but there's only a week left of summer, and then, quite possibly their relationship will be over.

"Sweetie?"

She turns around to see her dad standing in her doorway.

"Are you ready? Trevor is downstairs … waiting for you."

She nods. Then, she looks back at the mirror. *Here goes nothing.* After taking another breath to hold back her emotions, she turns and picks up her purse off her bed. She walks over to the door and kisses her dad on his cheek.

"Have fun tonight, and don't worry about what's happening this upcoming week, okay?" he says as he looks her in the eyes. "Promise me you're going to just enjoy yourself tonight."

She smiles softly and puts her hand over her heart as she nods. He kisses her cheek and then steps out of her way. Danielle holds her purse close to her as she walks out of her room and heads to the staircase, walking down. Once she reaches the bottom, she sees

Trevor and her grandma talking, giving her time to look at his outfit—a blue shirt with black pants and sneakers.

Trevor takes a quick glance at her but then looks back again and grins. He lets his eyes wander over her to check out what she's wearing—a flowy, spaghetti-strapped red V-neck shirt with blue jeans and flat summer shoes. Casual and comfortable, just what he suggested but she could wear anything and he'd love it. He raises his eyes to meet hers. She bites her lower lip. Trevor excuses himself from Grandma Marie before walking over to Danielle.

"You're beautiful," says Trevor as he lifts his hand and pushes her hair behind her ear before leaning in to greet her with a kiss. Then, he pulls back and whispers, "My beautiful girl."

She blushes. He knows how to get to her. She will miss that.

No. No. You promised Dad you would enjoy this. Don't think about it.

She smiles at him and mouths, *Thank you.*

"He's right, sweetie. You look beautiful," says Grandma Marie before she walks over to hug Danielle. Then, she whispers in her ear, "Have fun tonight. Don't let your thoughts stop you from having fun."

Danielle nods as she pulls back and looks back to see Trevor holding his hand out toward her, and she gladly accepts it.

"Ready to head out?"

She nods again, and Trevor tells Grandma Marie to have a nice night. He walks over and opens the front door for Danielle. Danielle walks outside with Trevor following close behind. She stares out to the street and opens her mouth in shock. There's a limo.

Is that for us? She's never ridden in a limo before, and she's hoping it is for them.

"Hope it's okay with you," says Trevor as he stands next to Danielle. "I wanted to focus on spending as much time with you as possible without driving. I asked my dad if we could borrow a limo from one of the hotels for the night."

Danielle turns to him and pulls him close to her, pressing her lips to his. She wraps her arms around his neck and runs her fingers through his hair. Trevor smiles against her lips before pulling away with a slight smirk.

Danielle strokes the hairs on the back of his neck as she mouths, *It's perfect.* Then, she pecks his lips.

Trevor smiles and takes her hand. He leads her down the porch steps and over to the waiting black stretch limo. The driver, dressed in a suit with a chauffeur hat, opens the back door. Danielle looks back at Trevor, and he nods. Then, she gets in and slides over, followed by Trevor. The driver closes the door.

Danielle gazes around the limo, amazed, until she feels Trevor's arm around her. She smiles as she scoots closer to him, so there's no space in between them. She shifts, so she can wrap her left arm around his torso as she snuggles against him. She wishes they could stay right there. Together. And not have to worry about next week.

Trevor looks down at the girl in his arms. He strokes her back as he rests his other hand on her cheek and then to her chin, so he can push her head up to connect their eyes. He runs his eyes over her face before reconnecting their eyes. He looks deep in them and knows what she wishes. He wishes the same. But right now, there's only tonight.

"Baby," he whispers as he leans his forehead against hers, "tonight ... tonight is all about you and me. We're not going to worry about tomorrow. It's all about right now. Okay?"

She bites her lower lip as she tries to hold back the tears threatening to form. Trevor slides his left hand down to her lower back and pulls her closer to him as he leans down to connect their lips. Danielle moans as she slides her left hand up from his torso to the back of his head and runs her fingers along his hair.

Neither notices when the limo starts to move. Trevor opens his mouth, and he uses his tongue to lick Danielle's bottom lip, asking for access. She opens her mouth, and he pushes his tongue between her teeth. He groans when his tongue touches hers, and they battle each other.

But when air is needed, Danielle pulls away and flutters her eyes open. She glances down at the smile on Trevor's lips, and she pecks his lips before resting her head on his chest. Trevor opens his eyes and looks down before shifting his body, so they can sit more comfortably. He keeps his hand on her lower back and strokes it as he puts his chin on her head.

This is all they need. Each other.

For one night, they forget everything.

THE LIMO DOOR OPENS, and Danielle pushes herself off of Trevor. Trevor stretches his arms before stepping out of the limo. Danielle slides over and sees Trevor holding his hand out toward her. She grabs his hand and steps out. She gazes around, realizing they're at the beach—the beach where they met, the beach where they spent most of their summer. She raises her eyebrow as she looks at Trevor for answers.

He turns her. "Let me guess ... you're wondering why we're here, right?"

Danielle nods.

"This beach has meant a lot to us. It's where we met, it's where we had our first kiss, and it's where I asked you to be my girlfriend." He laces their fingers together and gives her hand a slight squeeze as he stares in her eyes. "This is where we had many of our firsts, and I wanted to have our last date of summer here."

She grins. She then looks around the beach's parking lot and notices there aren't any other cars, so she looks back at Trevor, still confused.

"Oh. I also asked the people who run the beach if they could close the beach just for us," explains Trevor as he smiles but he sees her *what did you do* look. "Okay, so I might have paid them, but you don't need to worry about how much."

She puts up her hands in defense as she continues to grin. He takes her hand and leads her over to the walkway bridge that connects the parking lot to the beach. Once they walk over the bridge, Danielle looks at the quiet, sandy white beach and takes a breath of fresh air.

Trevor grins at her with a glint in his eyes. He knew this was a great idea. Just the two of them on *their* beach.

He pulls her along with him as they walk on the sand. Trevor stops and points over to the shoreline. She looks over and sees a table set for two with a flower bouquet in the middle of it and two covered plates. And when the time is right, they can watch the sunset together.

Danielle can sense tonight becoming the best last date she will ever have, but it also makes her sad, knowing that this also could be it. Done. It'll be over. She bites her lower lip as she shakes her head to clear those thoughts. She remembers once again that she promised her dad and her grandma that she would have fun tonight and not worry about what was coming.

"Come on," says Trevor.

They walk over to the table. Trevor pulls out one chair, and Danielle sits down. Then, he walks over and sits down on his own chair. Danielle gazes out to the water, noticing how peaceful and beautiful it is. There's no other place she'd rather be.

"Good idea?"

She looks at Trevor and enthusiastically nods.

"Good." He grins and leans over, so he can lift the cover off Danielle's plate to show a small pizza with pepperoni on top. "So, I figured since we enjoyed pizza this summer … it would be a good choice for our dinner—and without the mess."

Danielle giggles as she remembers the mess they created in the pizzeria. Even though that day ended up not being a great one, it's still one of her favorite days with Trevor from the summer—him trying to teach her how to make the pizza, the mess they ended up creating, and the way he kissed her. Trevor smiles as he, too, thinks back to that day.

"All right," says Trevor as he lifts his own plate cover, "Let's dig in."

TREVOR SITS on the beach towel he set up with Danielle sitting in between his legs as he has his arms wrapped around her. They watch the sun go down over the water, and this is their perfect, peaceful moment, where there are no words needed. Danielle turns her head to look at him, and he smiles down at her before leaning in to capture her lips with his own for a slow, gentle, but loving kiss. He then pulls back and kisses her nose.

"This is the best date I've ever had. No, scratch that. This has been the best summer I've ever had, and it's all because of you, Elle."

Tears form in her eyes. Danielle rolls over, so they are chest to chest. He watches her as she leans up to connect their lips together again. He's shocked at first, but he closes his eyes and kisses her back. Then, he lies back on his back, bringing Danielle down with him. He rests his hands on her lower back and strokes her back with his thumbs.

Danielle pulls back and pushes herself up on him. They stare at each other with love written in their eyes. But neither says those three words. The three words that could change everything. They both feel it, but they stay quiet as they hear the waves crash along the shoreline.

She's ready to speak, but something still holds her back. *I want to tell him. I need to tell him. Maybe, just maybe, we will last after next week.* But she bites her lower lip as the words won't come, and she doesn't understand why.

Danielle rests her head down against his chest to listen to his heartbeat. Trevor stares up at the now-dark sky and sees the stars starting to brighten down on them. He knows he should say those words. He wants to say them. But he holds back, knowing she won't say them back. He can feel her love, but selfishly, he wants her to tell him. He wants her to *say* them.

And she won't, so he won't.

TREVOR GRABS DANIELLE'S hand before they trudge up the stairs to the front door of her house. She turns to face him and takes her phone out of her purse. She smiles as she types something.

I had a great time. Are you coming over tomorrow?

Trevor reads her phone, and a fake smile forms on his lips. "Yeah. I'll come over around noon, okay?"

She nods and puts her phone away.

She bites her lower lip as she looks at him, waiting for a kiss, but he kisses her forehead instead before telling her, "Good night."

He turns around and walks down the stairs, away from her. Danielle watches him, and she wonders why he just walked away, but she lets it go.

Danielle turns around, walking inside, and sighs before heading up the stairs to her room. She thought this was one of the best nights of their summer and her life, but something changed in the last few minutes.

What happened?

TREVOR WALKS in his house and sighs, not knowing himself why he just walked away like that. Something inside of him hurts, and he knows he will not be able to handle it anymore. He needs her to open up to him and tell him how she feels—not just writing it down but telling him … with her voice.

He closes his eyes as he leans against the front door. He knows he's asking for a lot, and he's supposed to be understanding—and he is—but he can't leave her, knowing she feels the same way he does but won't tell him. He pushes himself off the door and heads up to his room to do what he's been doing every night that week—hoping for a better ending to summer.

Trevor and Danielle lie in their own beds as they think the same thing. *I love you.*

25

THE END?

*I*n three days, summer will be over, and Trevor will be on a plane to California, heading to Stanford. He and Danielle knew the day was coming but didn't expect it so fast. Two months have come and gone. Both wish they could go back to the day when they ran into each other on the beach, so they could relive the entire summer again. But it's not possible, so they plan to spend the last few days together.

"So … only a few days before summer's over," says Trevor quietly as he looks down at Danielle, her head lying on his chest.

She glances at him and sighs before looking back down. She uses her pointer finger to draw shapes on Trevor's shirt to distract herself. She doesn't want the end of summer to come. She's already lost one person she loved, and she's now close to losing another one. This time, she's losing the guy she has fallen in love with, and it scares her.

"Elle," asks Trevor as he strokes her hair, "are you okay?"

Danielle looks up and gives him a fake smile as she fights back the tears. Trevor shakes his head because he knows it's not a genuine smile. He gently pushes her off of him before getting off the bed, and he stands near the edge. She leans on her arms as she looks at him, confused.

"Why can't you be honest with me?"

She sits up and moves to the edge of the bed, and then she grabs her phone.

What do you mean?

"You know very damn well what I mean," says Trevor as he throws his arms up in frustration. "Why can't you tell me how you really feel about all this?"

Danielle looks down, knowing what he's talking about. Tears form in her eyes, but she won't let him see them. Ever since her mom died, she's been good at keeping her thoughts and feelings to herself, but it's getting harder and harder every day. Especially now.

Trevor walks over to her and kneels down in front of her, grabbing her hands. "Elle … I love you. And I'm willing to make this long-distance thing work."

She raises her eyes with a tear falling down her cheek. He said them. He said the three words she'd wanted to hear him say and the same words she wants to tell him. She loves him, and she wants to say them but she's not ready. She knows now what's holding her back, and it's because she's scared. The last person she said those words to died, and she's worried after saying them again to Trevor, things will just end badly. Where would that leave her?

"Baby … tell me how you feel." He strokes her cheek, wiping away her tear, but she ends up looking away, not answering, so he abruptly pulls his hands away from her. "I can't do this anymore." He stands up and steps back. "I'm done."

He walks over to her door and puts his hand on the doorknob.

He closes his eyes. He's ready to leave her room, her house, and her life … forever. It hurts. He hurts. And he knows what she's been through, but it's time for her to open up to someone, and he doesn't plan on sticking around forever, waiting to see if he will be that guy for her.

Tears are flowing down Danielle's cheeks as she stares at his back. She shakes her head. She can't believe that he's the same guy she fell in love with over the summer. She gets it. She understands, but it still hurts. Nothing will be the same from this day on. He's changed, and she noticed that before he left her on the front porch the other night.

Trevor opens his eyes and turns around sighing. "I love you and I always will. But … I can't handle the silence anymore. I want to be that person who you open yourself up to, but it doesn't seem like I am. I think this is for the best. I'm sorry. Have fun at Harvard."

With that, he turns away and pulls the door open. Then, he walks out, closing the door behind him. Danielle lets out a sob, and she covers her mouth as she falls back on-to her bed. She crawls up to lay her head on her pillow as she lets all her emotions out. She can't believe he walked out, and she let him. She let the one person who understands her go.

GRANDMA MARIE LIES on the bed with Danielle as she strokes her hair, trying to comfort her but nothing seems to be working. This is when Danielle could use a mom. But she knows Grandma Marie is the closest she has to one now. All she wants is comfort and answers as to why she just let him go. She's in love with him, and she wants him to know that, but it's still too hard for her to open up.

"Do you love him?" asks Grandma Marie as she continues to stroke Danielle's hair.

Danielle looks up at her and slowly nods her head as tears continue to fall. Grandma Marie pulls her close to her giving her a supportive and loving hug. She knows how hard it is for Danielle, but she also knows that it will only get harder if she doesn't tell him.

"Then, you need to tell him"—she pulls back and looks at her —"before it's too late. I know it's hard for you to open up because of your mom." She wipes away a tear off Danielle's cheek. "But you did this summer. To him. You let yourself be happy. You might have not realized it, but your dad and I did. And we couldn't be happier. But now you need to open up your heart and tell him. It's okay. Your mom would want you to. And I know you want to. It's time."

Danielle looks down and then glances at the clock sitting on her end table. She sees that she doesn't have much time left before his plane leaves. She looks back at her grandma.

"Go."

She hugs her grandma before jumping off her bed. Then, she pulls her door open and runs out of her room, down the stairs, and out of the house. This is it. She needs to tell him. It's time for Danielle Washington to speak again. She's ready, and all it took was for her grandma to tell her what she'd needed to hear.

TREVOR LOOKS DOWN while he sits in the back seat of his parents' car, waiting for the moment he's ready to get out and walk into the airport. He doesn't want to leave. He feels bad for what he did to Danielle, just leaving like that. There were so many times when he wanted to just text her or go over to her house and apologize, but he couldn't.

Joe turns around to face Trevor from the driver's seat and asks, "Are you all right, son?"

"I love her, Dad." He looks at his dad. "I really do. But this is for the best."

"Trevor, we've been meaning to talk to you," says Sarah as she turns to face him. "We just haven't been able to since you were busy or didn't want to talk."

"But we've seen those letters from Harvard in your room and understand you actually want to go there," says Joe. "Don't do this for us. I know we sort of pushed you to go to Stanford, but it's okay if you want to go to Harvard instead."

Sarah smiles softly as she finishes what Joe started, "We see how you feel about Danielle and you should do what makes you happy. It's not too late to change your mind. You can either transfer after the first semester or take the next six months off and then start in the spring."

"It's too late," says Trevor as he stares out the window. "I yelled at her. I told her I was done and just walked out. She didn't deserve any of it, but I said it anyway, and that's why I have to go. She hates me. This is what I have to do."

Joe opens his mouth to argue, but Trevor opens his door and gets out of the car. Joe and Sarah glance at each other before getting out of the car themselves. Sarah walks to the back of the car and reluctantly starts taking his bags from the trunk to keep herself busy. Joe walks around to the other side of his car and sees the distant look on Trevor's face, and he sighs again.

"I'll miss you, son." Joe walks over to him and puts his hand on Trevor's shoulder before hugging him. "You'd better call at least every other day, so we know how you're doing."

"I will." Trevor pulls back and turns to face his mom. "I'll miss you, Mom."

"My baby." Sarah tightly hugs him around his neck as tears form in her eyes. "I'll miss you, but have a wonderful time."

"I will," says Trevor as he pulls back and takes a breath as he looks at his parents. "But before I go … could you do one thing for me?"

Joe knows what he might ask, so he nods. "Sure, son. Anything."

"Can … can you tell Danielle that I love her and I'm sorry for how things ended?" asks Trevor, full of sadness.

Joe and Sarah nod their heads with sadness in their eyes. They both know their son is in love. They should have talked to him sooner, but nothing at the moment will change his mind about leaving. There is no way to stop him even though he might regret it.

"Thank you."

Trevor takes a deep breath and then picks up his carry-on and throws it over his shoulder. He grabs the handles of his two suitcases. He looks around and smiles at his parents before walking toward the door of the airport.

This is the right thing to do. There's no going back.

Before he takes a step through the automatic doors, he turns to his parents for one last time until he sees them again at Thanksgiving. But then he notices a taxi parking behind his parents' car, and he doesn't get why, but something tells him to wait. When the back door gets thrown open, he sees the wavy brown hair he loves running his fingers through before the girl he loves reveals herself.

Danielle presses her hand to the top of the door as she looks over at him with broken eyes. Then, she slams the door and turns away from the taxi. Trevor drops his bag on the ground and takes a few steps toward her. She stares at him before she runs over to him, jumping in his arms. He wraps his arms around her, and he puts his face in her neck, never wanting to let her go.

Danielle pulls back as her feet touch the ground and says the three words he's wanted to hear,

"I-I love you." She looks at him with tears in her eyes as she rests her hands against his chest. "I love you. D-don't g-go."

"You have no idea how good that sounds," he whispers as he presses his forehead to hers. "I love you too." He grins and then leans in to connect their lips for a gentle but passionate kiss. Then, he pulls back and puts his hands on her cheeks. "And I'm not going anywhere."

She stares at him, confused. "B-but Stanford?"

"I don't care about Stanford." He shakes his head as he uses the pads of his thumbs to wipe away her tears. "I care about you, and I'm not leaving you. My parents told me it's my choice, and I can start Harvard during the spring semester."

Danielle smiles as he continues to speak, "I was going to leave. But that was only 'cause I didn't think I deserved you after the other day, and I'm sorry about that. But right now, being with you is all I care about."

They look at his parents. Joe walks back to stand next to Sarah after paying the taxi driver. Sarah looks at them with happy tears flowing down her cheeks as she nods. She can't believe she and her husband were about to get in the way of true love. Joe puts his arm around her and pulls her close to him as he, too, nods.

Danielle looks back at Trevor. "I love you, Trevor."

"Okay, you really don't know how great that sounds. I love your voice. And I love you too," says Trevor as he smiles and slides his hands down her body to her waist, pulling her close to him so their bodies touch, "more than you can ever know."

Danielle grins as she moves her hands up from his chest to the back of his neck. She plays with the hairs on his neck as she pushes herself even closer to him, if possible. Trevor smiles down at her and closes his eyes as he leans in. She leans up to meet Trevor in the middle. Their lips touch to mark a new beginning.

This is proof that their love is more than just a summer fling. Before summer, Danielle would have never imagined finding love or even having a good summer, but from the moment he bumped into her on the beach, she thought Trevor would change her life for the better, and he did. They made it through the roller coaster of summer and came out stronger in the end.

Summer might have been a silent one, but the rest of their lives will be anything but.

AUTHOR'S NOTE

Dear Reader,

Thank you. Thank you. Thank you for reading *The Silent Summer*! I'm so happy it is finally out and in your hands. This has been an 11-year process. No joke. I started writing this story during my junior year in high school. I completed it during my senior year, but decided to take a couple years away and then just revised, revised, oh and revised some more with breaks in between before saying *It's done.*

When I started the process of coming up with the plot, I didn't want it to be just another summer love story. I wanted it to be different. But how? So, the first thing I thought about were the different ways people deal with their grief of a loved one, and went from there. I had Danielle choose silence as her way, but I didn't want her to be completely silent which is why I had her using her phone as a way of communicating.

There are a lot of meanings behind the three words, *I love you,* and they can be the hardest to say which is why I chose them to be Danielle's final words to her mom and the first to Trevor. Because when she said them, you know she meant them.

If you loved Danielle, Trevor, Jacob, and Grandma Marie, please consider leaving a review. I'd love to read your thoughts.

Want to stay in touch with me?

- Sign up for my Newsletter on my website.
- Subscribe to my YouTube channel.
- Join me on Patreon.
- Follow me on Goodreads, Facebook, Twitter, and Instagram!

Thanks again for your support!

Caitlin ❤

ACKNOWLEDGMENTS

I want to thank the following people because this book would never have happened without them:

- My parents for always believing in me and being supportive in anything I do, even if it did take years to get this book out. I love you.
- My sister, my brother-in-law (yes, even you), and my nephews for unknowingly distracting me when I needed it.
- My aunts, uncles, and cousins for always supporting me.
- My friends for always being by my side especially one of you who kept me in check when I got stuck or had doubts (you know who you are 'ultimate year').
- Jovana Shirley of Unforeseen Editing for taking my words and making them stronger, bringing out the best of the story.
- Jaycee DeLorenzo of Sweet 'N Spicy Designs for the awesome interior and cover design!
- My teachers, professors, and others in the Township of Union school system and at Kean University who have taught and helped me over the years.

ABOUT THE AUTHOR

Caitlin Goerlich writes contemporary romance. She received her Bachelor's Degree in English with a focus on Creative Writing from Kean University.

At a young age, Caitlin was diagnosed with kyphoscoliosis (an abnormal curvature in the spine) which lead her having complications in surgeries causing her to have spinal nerve damage and becoming a paraplegic. Her official diagnosis is spinal cord injury.

When Caitlin is not writing, she is enjoying life by competing in adaptive sports, spending time with friends & family, recording videos for her YouTube channel, motivational speaking, and being chairperson and board member of the Tri-State Wheelchair Athletic Association board.

To find out more about Caitlin Goerlich, go to
www.caitlingoerlich.com
or follow her by using the links below.
www.youtube.com/TheCGoerlich
www.patreon.com/CGoerlich
www.twitter.com/CGoerlich
www.facebook.com/WriterCaitlinGoerlich
www.instagram.com/CGoerlich
www.goodreads.com/CaitlinGoerlich

CPSIA information can be obtained
at www.ICGtesting.com
Printed in the USA
BVHW042003250521
608124BV00010B/66